3.50

THE FAMOUS FIVE AND THE STRANGE SCIENTIST

THE FAMOUS FIVE are Julian, Dick, George (Georgina by rights), Anne and Timmy the dog.

Despite his reputation for eccentricity, the behaviour of the brilliant scientist staying at Kirrin Cottage puzzles the Five. Is he an imposter? And if so, where is the real Professor?

The Five's suspicions lead them into an unexpected encounter with an international spy-ring and a thrilling adventure on their own doorstep.

Also available from Knight Books:

The Famous Five and the Strange Scientist

A new adventure of the characters created by Enid Blyton, told by Claude Voilier, translated by Anthea Bell

Illustrated by Bob Harvey

KNIGHT BOOKS
Hodder and Stoughton

First published in France as *Les Cinq Jouent Serré*

First published in Great Britain by Knight Books 1985

British Library C.I.P.

Voilier, Claude
The Famous Five and the strange scientist.
I. Title II. Les Cinq jouent serré. *English*
843'.914[J] PZ7

ISBN 0-340-36810-1

Printed and bound in Great Britain for Hodder and Stoughton Paperbacks, a division of Hodder and Stoughton Ltd., Mill Road, Dunton Green, Sevenoaks, Kent (Editorial Office: 47 Bedford Square, London WC1B 3DP) by Hunt Barnard Ltd., Aylesbury, Bucks.

CONTENTS

Chapter One

A SCIENTIST COMES TO STAY

George and her cousins were playing on Kirrin beach, down below Kirrin Cottage, the seaside house where she lived with her parents, Aunt Fanny and Uncle Quentin. They were Julian, Dick and Anne's very favourite aunt and uncle, because they always let the three children come to Kirrin to spend their holidays with George, whose real name was Georgina. Just at the moment all four cousins were jogging along the beach abreast of each other, passing a big football. It wasn't really just a silly game – it called for a good eye and careful judgement, and the Five liked to keep fit. Yes, there *were* five of them – the fifth was George's beloved dog Timmy, who was racing along level with the breakers as fast as he could go, barking like anything at the seagulls to chase them away.

'Timmy, don't!' Anne told him. 'After all, the

sea's their home! You wouldn't like it if they came and tried to peck you out of your nice warm basket in Kirrin Cottage!'

When they had all had enough of their game, the children sat down on the smooth yellow sand, and Timmy came to lie beside his little mistress, panting hard.

'Oh, I'm so glad it's the holidays!' said George. 'We can play, and bathe, and go out in my boat, and have all the fun we want!'

'Yes – but we won't have the beach to ourselves all the time, like today!' said Julian. 'So let's make the most of it before any tourists arrive. School broke up early this term, but there'll soon be a lot of other people on holiday coming to Kirrin.'

'And don't forget those scientists!' said Dick. 'Though I don't suppose *they* will want to play football on the beach.'

'You mean the scientists coming for their – their comparence?' asked Anne, trying to get her tongue round the difficult long word.

George and Dick rolled about on the sand laughing, which wasn't really very kind of them. Julian smiled encouragingly at his little sister.

'Conference, Anne – the word's conference!' he told her.

'Yes, so it is! *Conference*,' said Anne, concentrating hard. 'I know what a conference *is*, anyway. It's a kind of meeting of lots of scientists, and they're having one in the town of Trentingham, not far away from Kirrin.'

'Not just any old scientists, either!' Dick pointed out. 'They're the absolutely first-class most brilliant scientists in the whole world, and their countries are sending them to the conference at Trentingham so they can compare notes, and discuss their research and inventions, and – and so on, in peace and quiet.'

There was a sparkle in George's eyes. 'I've got a surprise for you, too!' she told her cousins. 'You know my father – the famous Quentin Kirrin, as the newspapers describe him – is going to the conference, but here's something Mother and Father only told me this morning. There are going to be so many scientists that the Trentingham hotels and guest-houses won't have room for them all, so some of them are going to stay in private houses. And the most famous of the lot is coming to stay *here*, at Kirrin Cottage! My father's been wanting to meet him for ages and ages!'

George's three cousins all sat up and took notice.

'What – a foreign scientist, coming to stay at Kirrin Cottage?' said Dick.

'Yes, and not just any old foreign scientist either! It's Professor Nicholas Kolkov in person!'

Even Anne had heard of the famous Professor Kolkov. He had been born in Varania, a little Central European country, and his name was now known all over the world. People said there were two things he really loved: his son Alex and Scientific Discovery (with a capital S and a capital D!)

'His son is coming with him, too,' George went on. 'They've never been to England before, and they're both of them staying with us. Alex Kolkov is seventeen.'

'I don't suppose that's too old to kick a ball about or enjoy a dip in the sea!' said Dick. 'I hope we'll make friends with him.'

'Only if he's a bit more sociable than his father,' said George. 'Apparently the Professor is a very abrupt, surly sort of character, and hardly ever says a word to anyone outside his work.'

'What fun!' groaned Dick. 'Why on earth did Uncle Quentin want to invite him, then?'

'Because it's his work he's interested in, I expect,' said George. 'You know how wrapped up my father is in his own clever scientific researches! And underneath that prickly manner, the Professor is said to have a heart of gold.'

'Well, let's look on the bright side,' said Julian, sensibly, 'and hope that he and his son will like *us*! I mean, friendship isn't all one way, is it? Now then, come on, who's coming in the water?'

Everyone was! The Five ran into the sea, splashing and shouting and – in Timmy's case – barking happily.

Next day the four cousins watched the news on television to see the Kolkovs arrive at London Airport. They looked at the old scientist coming down the steps from the plane with great interest. Soon he would be staying in this very house!

'He does look a bit gruff!' said Anne, under her breath. She thought for a moment, and added, 'Rather like a big grizzly bear!' Certainly, the Professor *was* something like a bear, with his great shock of hair and his bushy eyebrows, and the gruff voice in which he replied to the reporters' questions.

'But I think he's nice,' said Anne, after a moment.

'Of course he's nice,' said Dick confidently. 'Almost as nice as his son!'

Young Alex Kolkov was standing beside his father and smiling. He was a slight, fair-haired boy, with rather a dreamy look in his eyes. The television picture gave the children a good look at the people coming off the plane – and when a reporter spoke to the Professor and his son at some length, they were pleased to find that both of them spoke fluent English!

'They're going to spend the rest of today and tonight in London,' George told her cousins. 'And tomorrow my father and two of the other scientists are going to meet them at Trentingham station. See how interested all those reporters are! That's because the Professor hardly ever leaves his native country.'

'Do you think Uncle Quentin will let us go to the station too?' asked Julian.

'Yes, of course, my boy!' said Uncle Quentin, coming into the room just as he spoke. 'Come by all means, if you'd like to – but there won't be room for everyone in the car, so some at least of you had better cycle to Trentingham. It'll be good exercise!'

Well, the Five never minded exercise, or a bicycle ride! They decided they would *all* bicycle to Trentingham station, and keep in the background while the official reception committee welcomed Professor Kolkov and his son. Afterwards, as they were pedalling back to Kirrin Cottage, George told the others what she thought about the new arrivals. 'I was a bit disappointed, really,' she admitted. 'I didn't think the flesh-and-blood Kolkovs looked quite as nice as they'd seemed on television!'

'Oh, come on, George!' said Julian. 'You couldn't possibly tell! Why, we only got a glimpse of them at the station – we'll get to know them much better once we're back in Kirrin, and *then* we can decide if we like them or not!'

When the children got back to Kirrin Cottage, Aunt Fanny had just made a nice pot of tea, and she and Uncle Quentin and their guests were sitting down to drink it. The children were

introduced, and the Professor and his son shook hands warmly with them. The old scientist even patted Timmy, and Alex smiled at the Five in a very friendly way.

After the Kolkovs had unpacked, it was lunch-time. Aunt Fanny had made a delicious lunch of roast lamb, with strawberries and cream for pudding – she said she wanted her guests to have English food at its best, but the children somehow doubted that the Professor noticed what he ate at all, any more than Uncle Quentin did! The two scientists were soon deep in discussion of something the children couldn't understand a bit. 'Talking shop again!' sighed Aunt Fanny, shaking her head at her husband.

After a while, however, the children changed their minds: Uncle Quentin was certainly deep in discussion, yes! But the Professor only listened, or said a brief 'Yes' or 'No', shaking his head. Of course, they remembered, he had a reputation for being rather gruff.

Alex made up for it by being really friendly to the children. They were all several years younger than he was, but he didn't seem to mind that. Julian and Dick took to him straight away. Anne thought he was very good-looking, and listened admiringly to everything he said. George was the only one who didn't feel quite at ease with him.

She couldn't work out just why. 'I think he's sort

of overdoing it,' she told her cousins later, when the Five were alone again. 'His father is just as gruff and abrupt as we'd heard, but Alex – well, he's almost *too* friendly!'

Dick burst out laughing. 'Honestly, George, you're the end! What *does* the poor thing have to do to please you? I think Alex is a really good sort. I can tell you, there are some boys of seventeen who would think themselves much too grown-up to talk to us and be so friendly. He's not a bit stuck-up, even though his father is such a famous scientist.'

'Well, so is *my* father a famous scientist, and you haven't noticed *me* being stuck-up, have you?' said George. 'I only meant that Alex – '

'Woof!' Timmy interrupted her.

George looked at her dog. His eyes were shining, and he was wagging his tail like anything.

'He's reminding you Alex gave him a biscuit!' Anne said, laughing.

'Oh, all right, all right!' grumbled George. 'I get the idea! You mean I'm the only one who doesn't take to the marvellous Alex! I give in! He's wonderful, terrific, and we're going to be bosom pals with him. Everyone satisfied now?'

In spite of George's sarcasm, her cousins *were* very friendly with the young visitor before two days were up. Alex spent almost all the time with the children. He had hired a bicycle, and went cycling round the countryside with the Five. They showed him Kirrin, and took him down to bathe on the beach with them, and they went out in Kirrin Bay for a row in George's boat. He seemed to enjoy it all very much.

Yet all the same, living in such close contact with Aunt Fanny and Uncle Quentin's two guests, George couldn't help feeling a little uncomfortable when she was with them. It was really very odd! As if there were something strange and almost unreal about the two of them!

'I expect it's because they're foreign,' Julian said sensibly, when she mentioned this feeling of hers to him. 'I mean, we never met any Varanians before. But – well, you know, I see what you mean, George. There are moments when *I* feel rather awkward with them too, though I don't know why.'

'The fact is, I feel the same!' Dick admitted. 'I've tried to tell myself it's nonsense, but it's no good – I get the impression there's something bogus about Alex. I mean, I know that sounds silly, but that's the word to describe the way *I* feel.'

George frowned. Yes, it was certainly strange, but she had got the same impression too. How could Alex be bogus, though? Perhaps it was just that he was trying specially hard to be polite to his hosts, and not knowing English ways, he overdid it!

Then she felt cross with herself. 'We really can't

hold his friendliness against him, can we?' she muttered to herself.

Anne and Timmy, however, still liked Alex just as much as ever. In Timmy's case it was cupboard love – Alex kept feeding him biscuits and sugar lumps!

But it wasn't long before the Five had something else to occupy their minds – something rather intriguing.

Chapter Two

THE PROFESSOR'S SECRET

The Five had gone out into the garden of Kirrin Cottage after breakfast. Uncle Quentin and Professor Kolkov had just set off for Trentingham and the conference, and Alex had gone up to his bedroom.

It wasn't often that the four cousins were at a loss for words – but they all looked at each other for several moments without opening their mouths! Then, at last, Dick asked, 'I say – did you notice anything *funny* about anyone, at breakfast?'

'Yes, I did!' Anne said at once. 'Professor Kolkov didn't – well, didn't seem his usual self!'

'Anne's right,' agreed George. 'He looked different somehow.'

'Yes, but different *how*?' wondered Julian. He was looking thoughtful. 'He was wearing the same clothes he had on yesterday and the day before.'

'No, it was his *face* that seemed different,' said Anne.

'That's right,' Dick agreed with his sister. 'There *was* something different about his face.'

'And again, *what* exactly was the difference?' said Julian, frowning. 'Do you think he usually wears false teeth and he forgot to put them in this morning? That makes a difference to the shape of a person's jaw.'

'No, we can rule that out!' said Dick. 'We'd have noticed if his teeth were missing all right. Anyway, he crunched up several slices of toast, very noisily, and you can't crunch toast without any teeth! Let's think – had he got a swollen cheek or a black eye or anything like that?'

'We'd have noticed a black eye all right, too!' said George 'Oh – wait a moment! I've got it! It was his hair!'

'Yes!' cried Anne. 'He'd just brushed his hair a different way, that's all. Well, there isn't any mystery about *that*!'

'We can have a good look when he and Uncle Quentin get home this evening,' said Dick cheerfully. 'Come on – let's call Alex down and go for a bathe in the sea!'

So the four children went and stood under Alex Kolkov's window and called to him. Smiling, he leant out of the window, which was surrounded by ivy.

'I'm terribly sorry, I can't come down to the beach with you today,' he said. 'I'm not feeling very well, or maybe I'm just a bit tired – but anyway, I think I'll just spend the day reading in my room. You don't mind, do you?'

Of course the Five were sorry he wasn't feeling well, but they went off to bathe without him. Alex did come downstairs at lunch-time, however. His father and Uncle Quentin weren't there, of course; they would be in Trentingham with the other scientists at the conference all day.

After lunch the children went out to the kitchen to offer help with the washing up. It had suddenly occurred to them that having the Kolkovs staying meant quite a lot of extra work for Aunt Fanny.

'Thank you very much, but that's all right!' said Aunt Fanny, laughing. 'You run out and enjoy yourselves – after all, you're on holiday! As for *you*, Timmy, I know your way of helping with the washing up only too well. You think licking the plates clean will do it. Now then, Dick, you can leave those sugar lumps alone – anyone would think you hadn't had two helpings of cold ham and salad and two helpings of trifle for lunch! Why don't you take Alex and show him the old church? I'm sure that would be interesting for him.'

'Alex doesn't feel like going out today,' said Julian. 'He stayed in his room all morning.'

Aunt Fanny was surprised. 'Are you sure?' she

said. 'Or did my own eyes deceive me? I thought I saw him go out of the side gate as soon as you children had left. Not that it matters – off you go and enjoy the sunshine!'

The Five gathered out in the garden again. George was rather intrigued.

'Well, how odd!' she said. 'If my mother was right, Alex lied to us. But what on earth for?'

'Maybe he's bored with us and thinks we're just little kids!' said Julian feeling rather annoyed. 'He's seventeen, after all!'

'But that doesn't explain his lying,' said George.

'No,' Dick agreed. 'He only had to tell us straight out! We're quite old enough to understand if somebody wants to be alone for a change.'

'He really *is* an odd character,' muttered George.

'Oh, come on, George – don't let your imagination run away with you! If you start scenting a mystery –'

'But you *know* I'm good at scenting out mysteries, Dick!' said his cousin. 'Almost as good as you are at scenting out rabbits, Timmy, aren't I?'

'Woof!' said Timmy firmly. And he wagged his tail, to let his mistress know he wanted to go for a walk.

It wasn't until that evening at supper-time that the four cousins remembered their conversation that morning. Seeing old Professor Kolkov sitting opposite them, they had a good chance to notice the difference in his appearance. They gulped down their pudding – a delicious summer pudding, too! – so as to get up to the boys' room and be able to discuss it in peace.

'It *was* his hair,' said Anne. 'He's done it differently.'

'No, he hasn't,' George contradicted her. 'His hair is exactly the same as usual.'

'Then what *is* it that's different?' wondered Julian, baffled.

'It's his forehead, Ju!'

'His *forehead*? But a person's forehead can't change, unless you comb your hair over it in a fringe, and Professor Kolkov's great mop of hair certainly doesn't fall in a fringe.'

'All the same, his forehead is lower than usual!'

'It can't be!' said Julian.

'It is, though,' George insisted. 'That was one of the very first things I noticed about the Professor – his enormous, high forehead. And today it's a low one!'

'Perhaps it shrank in the wash!' said Dick, laughing at his own joke.

It certainly *was* a puzzle, but they had to leave it there for the time being, and anyway there was an exciting television programme they all wanted to watch, so they forgot about it until next day.

Next day, however, they had another surprise. Professor Kolkov's forehead was back to normal!

'Amazing!' whispered Dick. 'It goes up and down! Like the tide coming in and out!'

'Ssh!' Julian whispered back. 'He'll hear you!'

But Professor Kolkov didn't seem to be listening, and he and Uncle Quentin were soon off in the car on their way to Trentingham again. Today Alex was obviously feeling better, or not so tired, whichever had been wrong with him, because he stuck to the Five like a limpet. Realising that George wasn't being very forthcoming, he tried to get back into her good books by asking her questions about her father's wonderful scientific discoveries and saying how much he admired them. She replied rather vaguely, and without much enthusiasm.

'George, you're not being very nice to him!' Anne told her in an undertone, a little reproachfully.

'Well, I can't help it,' said George, crossly. 'He's getting me down! I tell you what, I think he's sucking up to us – and what's more, I think he's a lot too inquisitive!'

That evening Dick suggested a trip in George's rowing boat, and when they were out on the sea in it he said he wanted to be sure no one else could overhear what he had to say. 'So I thought this was the safest place!' he added. 'Right – George thinks there's something odd about the two Kolkovs. I don't know if she's right or not, but personally I'd like to know more about the Professor. So I'm going to set about it tonight!'

'Set about what?' asked his brother, worried.

'I'm going to find out what he does when he's alone in his bedroom!' said Dick.

'Oh, Dick! You can't go spying on a guest!' protested Anne. She didn't like the idea any more than Julian did. 'Think how cross Aunt Fanny and Uncle Quentin would be!'

'Yes, I know. But if there really *is* a mystery about the Professor, we want to know what it is, don't we?'

'Yes, we do!' George agreed firmly.

And Timmy barked, too. 'Woof, woof!' He was on their side.

'So when the Professor has finished talking to Uncle Quentin and goes up to his room,' Dick went on, 'I'm going to –'

'Look in through the keyhole, I expect!' said Julian, grinning in spite of himself. 'Bet you can't see anything!'

'No, no, Ju! There's a little balcony outside the Professor's bedroom window, remember?' said Dick. 'He never draws his curtains, because that room looks out over the garden. Well, I'm going to climb up to the balcony and look in at the window!'

'Suppose somebody catches you?' said poor

little Anne, feeling worse than ever about the whole idea.

'Nothing ventured, nothing gained! Ever heard of *that* saying?' Dick asked. 'I just want to see if Professor Kolkov goes in for fancy hairdressing when he's on his own in front of his mirror, or if he's got a kind of extending forehead!'

Julian and Anne looked at each other – but it was only too obvious that nothing *they* could say would stop Dick carrying out his plan. The Five were always loyal to each other, so Dick's brother and sister were there too when he, George and Timmy slipped quietly out of the house that evening.

'I'm going to climb the ivy,' Dick told the others in a whisper. 'It's quite strong enough to support me.'

And he started to climb. The others stood in the shelter of the trees below as he made his way up to the little wooden balcony, cautiously approached the window, and peeped in.

A moment later Dick was on his way back down the ivy, with a broad smile on his face.

'Ha, ha, ha!' he laughed, trying to keep his voice down – but something had amused him so much, it was difficult! 'Oh, what a joke! Know what *I* saw?'

'Not till you tell us, idiot!' said George. 'Come on, what was it?'

'Well, the learned Professor Kolkov, who's so

brilliant and clever and famous for his abrupt manner and all that, is really as vain as a peacock. I caught him in the act of taking his wig off! He's really as bald as a billiard ball! Ha, ha, ha! Oh, he did look funny! If only you'd seen him!'

After a moment of surprised silence, the other children began to laugh too. 'Well!' said Anne. 'If he's so vain he wears a wig to hide his bald head, I wonder why he chose *that* one? It's not a particularly handsome one, is it? If I were him I'd rather have had –'

'A pretty wig with long golden curls, I expect!' said Dick, teasing his little sister. 'Why don't you suggest it to him tomorrow? Ha, ha, ha!'

Julian and Anne couldn't help laughing again – but George didn't laugh. She had suddenly turned very thoughtful, and she was frowning.

'What's the matter, George?' asked Julian. 'What are you thinking about?'

'Actually, it struck me that what Anne said wasn't so silly after all,' said George. '*Why* didn't Professor Kolkov pick a more ordinary sort of wig?'

'I expect it was because his own hair was as shaggy as that wig *before* he went bald,' said Julian. 'And so he wanted a wig that would make him look the same as before. People can go bald quite suddenly, you know.'

'Yes, that *might* explain it,' said George, but she still looked rather thoughtful. 'However, that's not the only thing bothering me – there's something else, if I could only think what! Wait a minute . . . yes, *that's it*! Of course!'

Her eyes were wide with surprise as she looked at her cousins.

'Professor Kolkov can't *possibly* be bald!' she told them.

Julian, Dick and Anne just stared at her, baffled. 'Why not?' asked Julian.

'Don't you remember – all the newspapers and television reporters have been going on about the scientists at the Trentingham conference for days, describing the various discoveries they've made. And one of the things they mentioned was that years ago, when he was still quite young, Nicholas Kolkov hit the headlines by discovering a cure for baldness. After that he went on to make a lot of much more important discoveries, but the baldness cure was famous, and now there aren't any bald men in Varania at all. Unfortunately the Varanian government refused to let any other countries have the formula – but that's another story. To come back to *this* one: Professor Kolkov actually *discovered* a cure for baldness. So how *can* he be bald himself?'

'Well, he is!' stated Dick. 'George, I saw it with my own eyes. I expect he adjusts the wig from time to time, and that's what makes his forehead look higher or lower!'

But George stuck to her guns. 'I tell you, he *can't* be bald!' she insisted.

'Perhaps he doesn't want to try his own cure! Perhaps he *likes* being bald?' said Julian.

'Yes, Julian, I'm sure you're right,' said Anne.

George only shook her head. 'Then why wear a wig?' she said, as she followed her cousins back into the house. 'I can't make it out at all – can you, Timmy?'

'Woof!' barked Timmy quietly.

However, there was nothing else she could think of to explain the oddity! And as the children were tired, they all went to bed – though it was a long time before George could drop off to sleep as she lay there puzzling over the mystery of the bald Professor.

She found it was still on her mind when she woke up the next morning, but her cousins seemed to have forgotten about it. And anyway, they discovered something else odd next day – something odd about Alex Kolkov, this time!

Chapter Three

HOW OLD IS ALEX?

Timmy had decided to do a bit of showing off. The children and Alex were playing with a football on the beach, when Timmy joined in! He caught the ball in his front paws, got it standing still, and then climbed on top of it and managed to move it along without falling off, just like a circus dog.

This was the latest trick George had taught him, and he and she were both very proud of it. Alex admired the clever dog.

'He's really great, George!' said the young Varanian. 'I like your Timmy! You know, he reminds me of a dog I got for my tenth birthday a dozen years ago. My uncle bought her from a family of travelling tinkers who'd trained her. She could walk along on top of a ball just like Timmy, and she could jump through a paper hoop too!'

'Oh, George – that would be another good trick

to teach Timmy!' cried Anne. 'He's so intelligent; I'm sure he'd learn it quite quickly.'

'I'll think about it,' said George.

But she was obviously thinking about something quite different – and when they all went into the water for a swim, to cool off after their game of ball, she waited for Alex to be out of earshot. He was a strong swimmer, and soon struck out for the rocks some way off. George swam up to her cousins.

'I say – did you hear what he said just now?' she asked them. 'It was rather funny, wasn't it?'

Dick and Anne didn't follow her at all, and asked what she meant. But it was Julian who told them.

'Yes, it *was* funny,' he agreed. 'Alex told us he got a dog for a tenth birthday present, a dozen years ago.'

'Well, what's so odd about that?' asked Dick, still baffled.

'Ten plus twelve makes twenty-two, that's what's odd about it,' his brother told him. 'Twenty-two, not seventeen!'

'Hm – yes. All right, Ju, I know you're brilliant at arithmetic!' said Dick laughing, and splashing his brother. 'Yes, Alex *is* seventeen! Well, maybe he just got the date wrong?'

'People sometimes say "a dozen" when they don't actually mean twelve,' Anne suggested, treading water.

'But if Alex is really seventeen, and he got the dog for his tenth birthday, 'half a dozen years' would be more like it,' George pointed out. 'That's what he'd have said if he meant it as just a vague, round number!'

'Well then, perhaps he wanted to make out he was older than he really is, so as to seem grown up,' said Anne.

'No, that's not like him,' said George decidedly. 'I think it's the other way round. He's making out he's *younger* than he really is!'

Her cousins all looked very surprised. 'Hang on, George!' said Dick. 'You're crazy! You were quoting the newspaper reports yourself just now. Well, they all said Alex Kolkov was seventeen. Seventeen years old, that's what they said!'

'Yes, I know!' said George. 'But actually, it's not the first time I've got the impression Alex is really older than he says.'

'But *why* –' Julian began.

At that moment, however, they saw Alex turn and begin to swim back from the rocks, and they had to stop discussing him!

However, they kept on wondering about it all morning. If Alex was older than he and everybody else said, why pretend to be younger? There didn't seem to be any point in it, especially when you had to suppose the newspaper reporters had agreed to pretend the same thing too! However, now that the children looked at Alex again they did spot some clues they hadn't noticed before. Alex shaved carefully every day, and seemed to have a much stronger growth of beard than you'd expect on someone of only seventeen. And now and then the way he spoke and acted was more like a grown-up than a teenager.

In fact, the children found that their suspicions of Alex were growing. And then another thing happened to increase the mystery that surrounded the two Kolkovs! It was something rather surprising – Professor Kolkov himself shattered his reputation for having a heart of gold under a gruff exterior.

It happened to be Sunday, so the scientists didn't have to go to Trentingham for one of the conference meetings or lectures as usual, and Professor Kolkov was sitting in the garden having a little nap. Aunt Fanny, smiling indulgently, told the children not to disturb him. However, Timmy can't have been listening to her. The four children were going down the garden path as quietly as they could, to go out of the gate, when the dog suddenly seemed to get wind of the Professor, broke away from his mistress and dashed towards the sleeping man, barking loudly! Perhaps he only wanted to say a friendly 'Hallo!' but his barks woke the Professor, who wasn't at all pleased. Muttering something cross in his own language, Professor

Kolkov gave poor Timmy a savage kick. The dog yelped in pain.

It all happened so fast that George had no time to do anything. But when she heard her beloved Timmy howling like that she rushed towards him, followed by her cousins. The scientist had obviously thought he and the dog were alone, because he looked a bit embarrassed and confused.

'I do apologise,' he said. 'I was asleep – that dog of yours woke me up all of a sudden, and I kicked out without really thinking.'

Nobody said anything. Timmy had run to George and was keeping close to her, with his tail between his legs. The Five all hurried off down to the beach. George could hardly contain her fury, and once they were out of earshot of the Professor she exploded!

'Well! Did you ever see anything like *that*?' she said. 'The brute! Fancy kicking Timmy!'

'He did say he was sorry and he hadn't thought first,' Anne timidly pointed out, for she was a very fair-minded little girl.

'He had plenty of time to think! He woke up and swore at Timmy before he kicked him,' said George.

'Yes, he did it on purpose,' Dick agreed. 'And he looked as if he enjoyed doing it, too! As if he got a kick out of it!'

But nobody laughed at this terrible joke! George

was far too upset for that, and so were the others. The two girls felt Timmy all over to make sure there was no real damage done. Timmy rather liked being the centre of so much attention, and decided to let out a few yelps and whines! But Julian saw through that.

'Now then, Timmy, you're not dead yet!' he said briskly. 'But I think you'd better avoid the Professor in future! Right?'

Oh dear – when Julian said 'Right', Timmy must have thought he said, 'Bite', because his pathetic whine changed to a furious growl. He was obviously about to take off and dash back to Kirrin Cottage and nip his enemy's ankles, but this time George was in time to stop him.

'No, Timmy! Heel!' she said firmly, even though she couldn't help smiling. 'We're not going in for any pitched battles. But I haven't forgiven Professor Kolkov, all the same.'

'Woof!' said Timmy. It was quite clear that he meant *he* hadn't forgiven the Professor either, and all the children laughed!

However, Julian soon turned serious again. 'It *is* odd, all the same,' he said, shaking his head. 'That was a really nasty thing for Professor Kolkov to do. And he's supposed to have such a kind heart in spite of his brusque ways!'

'Personally, *I* haven't noticed it,' said Dick. 'The kind heart, I mean. I've heard him speak quite sharply to his own son, several times!'

'Yes – and the other day, when Joan came up from the village to help Aunt Fanny clean the house, he spoke to her in a most *bossy* way!' said Anne. 'Ordering her about! Poor Joan – she was quite flustered and upset. *And* I saw him throwing stones at the nice tabby cat from the house next door, when it came to play on our lawn. He didn't know anyone was watching at first. Then he saw me, and that seemed to annoy him.'

'Altogether he's a nasty, brutal sort of character,' George decided. 'It sounds as if we were all beginning to suspect as much. And what we've just seen certainly shatters this idea that he's got a heart of gold!'

'Hear, hear!' said Dick. 'I tell you something – the better I get to know both the Kolkovs, the less I like them!'

So the children were not particularly pleased when Alex came to join their games next day. 'I say – why don't we go over to my island and play at being Robinson Crusoe?' George suggested.

'Good idea!' said Dick. 'I expect Aunt Fanny would let us take the tents and camp there for a few days, too. We haven't done that for ages – and it's nice fine weather at the moment. Yes, let's go to your island!'

'*Your* island, George?' asked Alex, sounding interested. 'Have you really got an island of your own? May I go camping with you too?'

Well, George could hardly refuse without being very rude, so she said, 'Yes, if you like. It's the island you can see from the beach, and it really does belong to me. My mother and father gave it to me for my very own. It's the best present anyone ever had!'

'I should think so!' said Alex. 'A real island!'

'It isn't a very *big* island,' George admitted, 'but it's got a stream of water, and a beach, and a nice sheltered little cove where we can leave the boat. And there are the ruins of an old castle on it. We can shelter there if it rains. You feel you're far away from the rest of the world on my island, though it isn't really all that far from the coast!'

'What fun!' said Alex. And it struck all the children that he was trying to sound childish, on purpose. 'I say – when can we start?'

'After lunch, if my mother says we can,' George told him. 'And we'll have to give her time to find us some provisions. We must get the tents and everything else ready, too.'

That didn't take so very long, and at about three in the afternoon the children, Alex and Timmy got on board George's rowing boat. It had been fitted with a sail quite recently, too, but they didn't put the sail up today, as there wasn't much wind.

The short voyage over, with Julian and Dick at the oars, was a smooth and easy one. They all got out on the little sandy beach, pulled the boat in, and then began carrying their tents and provisions to the place where they usually camped. Alex seemed delighted with everything: the green grass, the clear little stream, the steep cliffs on the seaward side of the island, the imposing ruins of the castle, the trees and the gorse bushes and the flowers. He liked it all. Timmy was rushing about like mad chasing rabbits – real or imaginary rabbits, nobody was quite sure which! Anne, like a good little cook, put all the food and the pots and pans neatly away in one of the ruined rooms of the old castle. She had improvised a sort of larder there. Dick built a fireplace for their camp fire, and Julian and George went to get water from the stream and collect dry sticks. Alex lent a hand willingly wherever he was needed.

In fact, he seemed to be enjoying it so much, and he really *was* being so helpful, and so happy to share the children's work, that they almost forgot their suspicions of him.

By evening the tents were all up, and supper was ready. Anne had made them a lovely supper of sausages, tomatoes and fried potatoes, and there were fresh cherries to follow – she had brought a little basket of cherries over in the boat.

When they had had all they wanted to eat, they sat around the camp fire singing songs. Dick played his mouth organ, and George and Alex told funny stories. At last, tired out and happy, they decided to go to bed – or rather, they decided to go to sleeping bag! George and Anne shared one tent, as usual, and Julian and Dick would have shared the other. But they had Alex to think of too. Julian said Alex could have his place in the tent, which would only take two, and he'd sleep outside, but Alex wouldn't hear of that. He said it was such a fine night that he'd be quite all right in a sleeping bag out in the open.

Soon the whole island seemed to be asleep. But Julian was lying awake. He didn't like to think that Alex hadn't got such good shelter for the night as the rest of them. After all, he *was* their guest! In the end he couldn't just lie there any more, and he got up very quietly, so as not to wake his brother, to go and make sure that Alex was really all right and comfortable in his sleeping bag.

The place where Alex had said he would sleep was a nice sheltered corner among the rocks, where soft green grass grew. The children had seen him unroll his sleeping bag and lay it down there. But when Julian got to the spot – the sleeping bag was empty!

Chapter Four

MORE MYSTERY

'I might have known it!' Julian muttered to himself. 'He couldn't get to sleep, so I suppose he's gone for a walk.'

Suddenly he heard a noise down on the little beach. Not a very loud noise – it was as if the person making it didn't want to be heard. And then, in the light of the moon, he saw Alex pushing George's boat out into the water again.

'Well, I suppose he's going for a row in the boat to make himself feel more sleepy,' thought Julian. But much to his surprise, he saw Alex rowing straight to the shore of the mainland.

'Perhaps he's going back to sleep in Kirrin Cottage, then,' Julian told himself. 'He must have been *very* uncomfortable! I wish he'd woken me – it isn't easy to handle the boat all alone.'

Suddenly Dick appeared by his brother's side. 'I

say, Ju – what's going on?' he asked, puzzled.

Julian pointed to the boat and Alex rowing it.

'My word – he's taken George's boat!' said Dick indignantly. 'Well, he might have asked first. I'm going to tell her!'

In a moment George and Anne had joined the boys. George didn't say a word at first – she just watched her boat being rowed away! Then she said, 'Alex is rowing very quietly, isn't he? As if he were taking great care not to splash or make any noise. It seems rather odd to me!'

'I don't see why,' objected Julian. 'Perhaps he just doesn't want to wake us up. You're always reading mystery into things, George!'

'Maybe I am,' said George, 'but I still want to know where he's going and what he does when he gets there! Come on! Let's follow him in the rubber dinghy!'

What luck they *had* an inflatable rubber dinghy! Uncle Quentin had given it to them last summer, so that they could get about on the water easily any time they wanted, without the trouble of launching the rowing boat. Being made of wood, of course the rowing boat was heavier to get ready and out into the water. And the Five had brought the rubber dinghy over to Kirrin Island with them, thinking it might come in useful. They pushed it out into the water and climbed into it. George and Dick took the oars, and in their own turn they rowed quietly towards the shore of the mainland. They didn't want Alex to spot them – but clouds had come up to cover the moon, and the rubber dinghy was dark-coloured, so it didn't stand out against the sea, while you could see the rowing boat quite easily because it was painted white.

'I say!' whispered Anne all of a sudden. 'Alex doesn't seem to be making for Kirrin Cottage!'

'No,' agreed Julian. 'He's rowing towards the cliffs – and now he's going ashore!'

Dick and George slowed down a bit, so as to give Alex time to get out of the rowing boat. They brought the dinghy ashore a little way off, but in the shelter of the same cliff. Just then the moon came out from behind the clouds again.

'Alex has vanished!' said Dick.

'Ssh!' hissed George. 'I can hear pebbles crunching – he must be going up the path between the beach here and the road.'

'Oh yes! I can see him now!' said Anne, who had very sharp eyes. 'He's almost at the top of the cliff now!'

'Let's follow him,' said George.

The four cousins and Timmy climbed the pathway up the cliff too, going in single file and being careful not to make any noise. They wondered why on earth Alex was behaving in such a strange way! What made him want to go off like this in the middle of the night? Well, they would soon know

now!

Once they got to the top of the cliff the Five turned right, bending low, and made for some gorse bushes which gave good cover, even if they *were* rather prickly. Alex still had his back turned to them, and obviously had no idea there were five silent shadows following him. He had stopped by the side of the road. Kirrin Cottage was on his left, about five hundred metres away, and he was looking in that direction.

'He seems to be keeping watch on something,' whispered Anne.

'Or on someone!' said Dick.

'Ssh!' said Julian and George together.

For at that very moment a dark shape appeared on the road. It was coming closer. Straining their eyes, the children made out the figure of a man pushing a motor-bike along. It was Professor Kolkov! He was puffing and panting as he came down the road – and Alex hurried to meet him.

The wind was blowing the wrong way for the children to be able to hear what they were saying. But from the word or so they *did* catch, they realised the Kolkovs were speaking Varanian, so they couldn't have understood the conversation anyway. Thanks to the moonlight, however, they could follow the gestures the two men were making as they talked.

Professor Kolkov handed the motor-bike over to

Alex, saying something which he followed up with an imperious wave of his hand. Alex nodded several times as he started the engine. Then he shot off into the night, bent low on the powerful bike, and his father started back to Kirrin Cottage. Alex passed quite close to the Five in their hiding place among the gorse bushes.

'He's turning off at the crossroads!' whispered Dick.

'Yes – and that's the road to Trentingham,' added George thoughtfully.

The children were disappointed. They hadn't really found out much. But the short scene they'd just watched gave them quite a lot to think about. Why were the two Kolkovs meeting in secret so late at night? Where had Alex gone? What had his father told him to do?

Lots of questions, but no answers so far! They couldn't follow Alex, who was well away on the motor-bike by now.

'What next?' wondered Julian. 'Shall we wait for Alex to come back, or shall we go back to the island?'

'Let's go back to the island,' said George. 'If we just stay here we're not likely to learn any more, and Alex may spot us on his way back. That would be silly!'

'Yes, let's go back,' Dick and Anne agreed.

Timmy was already dashing down the cliff path

again, just as if he understood. He was the first to jump into the rubber dinghy.

When they got back to Kirrin Island the four cousins went to bed again – but none of them could sleep much! They couldn't wait to find out what would happen next.

It was a long time before Alex came back. When he did, he slipped into his sleeping bag again as quietly as he'd left it. But the children were all awake and listening, and this time they heard him quite clearly, even though they all pretended to be asleep – including Timmy.

In the morning the children emerged from their tents to find the sun was already up and shining brightly. Alex came to meet them, looking very cheerful.

'Hallo!' he called happily. 'Sleep well? I did – I slept right through till dawn!'

It took Julian, Dick, George and Anne a lot of self-control not to exchange meaningful glances. Alex Kolkov certainly had a cheek – and he was a good actor, too!

The children hid their feelings as well as they could, and set to work to get breakfast. Toast made at a camp fire tasted extra delicious! Anne had opened a can of orange juice too, and fried some eggs and bacon. They were all very hungry after their night-time boating trip.

Dick had brought his little transistor radio over

to Kirrin Island with him, and he turned it on to listen to the news.

Suddenly, all the children froze, toast half-way to their mouths!

'Last night,' the newsreader was saying, 'a daring theft took place in the little town of Trentingham, where an important scientific conference is being held. One of the foreign scientists staying in Trentingham was robbed of an extremely precious document. The scientist, whose name we are not at liberty to reveal, never parted from this document, and always put it between his mattress and the bedstead before he went to sleep. Somehow or other the burglar managed to get into the scientist's bedroom, administer chloroform to make him unconscious, and then steal the document. At present the police have no clear leads.'

The children looked at each other.

'What a shocking thing to do!' said Alex, shaking his head seriously.

Four pairs of eyes turned to look at him. And then, fearing he might read their suspicions of him in those eyes, the children looked away again.

It wasn't until later that morning, while Alex was swimming about among the rocks, that the children got a chance to talk about it. They clambered into the rubber dinghy, which was bobbing about in the waves.

'Well – we all heard the news, didn't we?' said

Julian. 'A burglary in the middle of the night, just about the time when Alex was on the mainland!'

'And after we'd seen him ride off along the road to Trentingham,' said George.

'And he said he'd slept right through till dawn!' Anne remembered.

'And if we hadn't noticed anything he'd have had a perfect alibi!' finished Dick.

Obviously they all thought the same thing! George put it into words.

'Well, we agree, then, don't we? Putting two and two together, we come to the conclusion that Alex could easily have stolen that document!'

'*Why*, though?' asked Dick. In spite of the evidence, he wasn't quite happy with the idea. 'His father is one of the scientists at the conference! They're all working together!'

'But according to the radio newsreader, the document was a very secret, confidential one,' said Julian. 'So perhaps the scientist who was burgled wasn't going to let *everyone* know what was in it.'

'And you think that's why Professor Kolkov decided to steal it?' asked Dick. 'I suppose it's possible. But it's a bit much to swallow the idea of such an important scientist as the Professor *stealing* documents from one of his colleagues! I mean, Professor Kolkov doesn't need anybody else's discoveries to boost his reputation – he's quite famous enough already, thanks to his own!'

'Hm,' said George, thoughtfully. 'That sounds like good reasoning, Dick – unless Kolkov isn't a real scientist at all! Suppose he's a spy?'

This idea was like a bombshell! George's cousins looked at her in surprise.

'Not a real scientist at all?' asked Julian. 'Why, George, he's known all over the world!'

George shook her head impatiently.

'And he's known all over the world for having a lot of hair and a heart of gold and a son of seventeen, too!' she pointed out. 'Well, we've found out that he's really bald, and he's got a nasty nature, and a son of about twenty-two! Add the mysterious way he and Alex have been carrying on, and where does *that* get us?'

The other three just looked at her, bewildered.

'All right, I'll tell you,' she said. 'The more I think about it, the more likely it seems that Professor Kolkov and his son – if he *is* his son – are imposters! They're only pretending to be the real Kolkovs! Don't you remember how nice we thought Professor Kolkov and Alex looked when we saw them on television? But they seemed different, somehow, when we actually met them.'

'George, you're right!' whispered Anne. 'Oh dear – can it really be true?'

'Yes! Yes, I think it *can*!' said Julian, giving himself a little shake. 'Look at it that way, George, and it certainly explains everything!'

'As a matter of fact, George has only said out loud what I was beginning to think to myself!' claimed Dick. 'But it did seem such a fantastic sort of idea . . .'

'Woof!' agreed Timmy – and then he barked again, nose pointing out to sea. He was letting them know that Alex Kolkov – or the imposter pretending to be Alex Kolkov – was on his way back to them. The children took care to act as if nothing was the matter. Whatever happened, they mustn't let their companion know the suspicions they had of him!

Usually the Five rather liked to have adventures all on their own and leave grown-ups out of it. But this time such a serious crime had been committed that they knew they must tell the police. There was no doubt in any of their minds about that, and George said she would tell Uncle Quentin all about it that evening. Her cousins agreed that that was the best thing to do.

Anne had been told about the part the others wanted her to play – and at lunch she complained of a headache, and said she thought she might have a touch of sunstroke.

'Oh dear – I hope it's not too bad!' said Alex.

'All the same, I think we'd better go back to Kirrin Cottage,' said Julian, pretending to be worried. 'We can come back to the island for the night if you haven't got a temperature, Anne – but we'll leave it to Aunt Fanny to decide.'

Alex didn't suspect anything! Of course, Anne's 'sunstroke' was only an excuse for them to leave the island earlier than they'd planned. She kept saying her head ached as they all went back to Kirrin Cottage in the rowing boat, and in fact she wasn't lying – the sun *was* beating down very fiercely.

When they reached Kirrin Cottage Aunt Fanny gave Anne a nice cool drink and sent her off to lie down in her room. George said she'd keep the invalid company. Julian and Dick discovered a holiday task that they simply had to get done before the beginning of term – or so they said! The fact was, none of the children much wanted to be with Alex. They were afraid of giving themselves away to him!

The rest of the day seemed to pass very slowly. Timmy, like the faithful dog he was, stayed indoors with George and Anne instead of going for a nice run in the garden, so it was a long day for him, too. At long last Uncle Quentin and Professor Kolkov came home from Trentingham. Supper seemed to take ages, too, but at last it was over, and the two Kolkovs went up to their bedrooms for the night.

Julian, George, Dick and Anne waited a little longer before they went and knocked at Uncle Quentin's study door. Uncle Quentin always worked till late into the night – he said his brain was at its best then. He didn't seem very pleased to be disturbed by the children and Timmy.

'Well, children? What do you want at this time of night?' he asked. 'You should have been in bed a long time ago! And I'm in the middle of something very important!'

'Ssh, Father!' said George, putting a finger to her lips. Meanwhile Dick went over to close the window. 'We don't want anyone else to hear us! *This* is something very important too! Something we've just got to tell you!'

Chapter Five

A VISIT TO THE CIRCUS

'Yes!' Anne burst out. 'Professor Kolkov is really bald, and his son Alex is twenty-two, and he rides a great big motor-bike!'

Uncle Quentin's face was a picture as he looked at his niece!

'You certainly *have* got sunstroke, Anne!' he said. 'What on earth is all this?'

'It's perfectly true, Uncle Quentin,' said Julian, seriously. 'If you'll just listen to us for a moment you'll understand.'

And the children started to tell their story, not so excitedly now, and taking it in turns. At first Uncle Quentin said it couldn't possibly be true – but in the end he was convinced that there was, at the very least, a mystery which ought to be cleared up.

'So what you're really suggesting,' he said at last, 'is that our guests are imposters and have stolen secret documents – in fact, that they're spies! This is a very serious charge, you know, and we have no proof of it!'

'But we can get some!' cried George. 'All we have to do is set the Kolkovs a trap and put some suitable sort of bait inside it. Then we'll catch them in the act – always supposing they *are* guilty!'

'Well, well,' said Uncle Quentin thoughtfully. 'Julian, go and find your Aunt Fanny. I think we must all discuss this thoroughly.'

And Aunt Fanny and Uncle Quentin spent a long time that night talking to the children in an undertone, with the door of the study well shut. Timmy kept guard outside, ready to give warning if anyone – particularly either of the Kolkovs – came along. It was a real council of war! Everyone had a chance to say what they thought.

In the end a plan of George's was adopted, after a great deal of discussion and when some alterations had been made to it. The idea was that they would use a visit to the circus next evening as part of the plan. Everyone at Kirrin Cottage was already going – the rather grandly named 'World Circus' was passing through this part of the country, and was going to give a performance in Kirrin village. The Kolkovs had accepted an invitation to the circus with pleasure when Aunt Fanny and the children asked if they would like to go too. Apparently Varania was a rather austere little country where there wasn't much fun in the way of travelling circuses. As for Uncle Quentin, he couldn't really refuse to go with his guests, so *he* had already said he'd go to the circus performance too. When the arrangements were first made he had wished he needn't, but now he was glad of it.

The circus meant that everyone would be out that evening, and Kirrin Cottage would be empty. That was what George's plan depended on.

When Aunt Fanny, Uncle Quentin and the Five went to bed at last, they had it all worked out. Even though it was so late, Uncle Quentin had had a long telephone conversation with the Inspector at Kirrin police station. If the children's suspicions were correct, and the Kolkovs took their bait, then they would be well and truly caught!

Next morning seemed to the children to last for ever! Anne claimed to be well enough to come down for lunch at mid-day, and Uncle Quentin and the Professor were back from Trentingham just in time for the meal – there wasn't a session of the conference that afternoon, because it was a Saturday.

When they were all eating their pudding – a delicious lemon meringue pie – Uncle Quentin started the ball rolling.

'Professor,' he said, turning to his guest and sounding very pleased with himself, 'I haven't breathed a word of this at the conference meetings, because I didn't want to let anyone know until *I* was sure it would succeed, but I've just made a revolutionary new invention! It wasn't until I was working on it last night that I could be certain it would be all right – and now I *am* certain! I'm sure you can imagine how pleased I am. Just think – my plans can be used exactly as they now stand, although I'd rather work on the finer details a little more before I show them to the delegates from other countries attending our conference. I don't suppose I shall be taking out a patent on my invention before the end of the month.'

'Isn't that a bit risky, Uncle Quentin?' asked Julian. 'Suppose a delegate from some enemy country stole your plans before then?'

Uncle Quentin laughed in a carefree way.

'No danger of that, my boy! There's a good strong safe in my study, and anyway, who's to know the plans are in it? Once I've registered the formula for my invention it will be fully protected. Why – it could make me a small fortune in the commercial field alone!'

The two Kolkovs congratulated Uncle Quentin warmly.

'And my own country will benefit as well, so I'm all the more pleased!' said the Professor. 'I know our two countries have signed agreements to share the results of their scientific researches! Here's to your excellent work, and your successful invention!'

And the Kolkovs drank Uncle Quentin's health – but the children noticed them exchanging brief glances . . .

The Five met out in the garden as soon as lunch was over for a secret council of war.

'Well, everything's ready for the showdown!' said Dick. 'We've set the scene! Professor Kolkov knows there are valuable documents in Uncle Quentin's study.'

'And we didn't bait the trap too obviously, either,' said Julian. 'If the Kolkovs *are* what they say, it's perfectly natural for Uncle Quentin to have told them about his invention – his plans wouldn't have anything to fear from genuine patriotic Varanians!'

'We've really made things easy for them,' said George, smiling. 'An empty house at their disposal, and a safe which would take a bit of forcing, but we've let them know exactly where it is.'

'All I'm wondering is how Professor Kolkov will manage to leave the circus and get back to Kirrin Cottage,' said Anne.

'Don't worry – I'm sure he'll find a way,' said George.

'You know, I'm going to be quite disappointed if Professor Kolkov turns out to be genuine after all – heart of gold and all the rest of it,' said Dick. 'Wouldn't Uncle Quentin make fun of us!'

'We'll just have to wait for this evening to find out about that for sure,' said Julian philosophically. 'Then we'll see what happens.'

The big circus tent had been pitched in a field not far from Kirrin Cottage, so the children went on their bicycles while the grown-ups drove there in Uncle Quentin's car. The evening started very well indeed. The Five found they were enjoying the circus so much that they almost forgot about the trap they'd set for the Kolkovs. They had smuggled Timmy into the Big Top in a basket – the good dog kept very quiet, and seemed to be enjoying the show too. The 'World Circus' was a really good one. There were equestrian turns, jugglers, tight-rope walkers, acrobats, and they were all first-class artistes.

The party from Kirrin Cottage clapped each number loudly. Even Uncle Quentin, who was usually so stern and serious, laughed with the rest of them. As for Professor Kolkov, he seemed to be enjoying himself wholeheartedly, just like a little boy! Tender-hearted Anne felt ashamed she'd ever felt suspicious of him.

'How funny those clowns are!' the Professor said, turning to Aunt Fanny. 'We haven't got anything like this in Varania! Bravo, bravo!' he called.

Dick leaned over to whisper in George's ear. 'He seems to be enjoying the show without sparing a thought for those plans!' he said.

'Wait a bit!' George whispered back.

The first half of the show came to an end. Alex went to buy everyone ice creams in the interval, and the children felt they had to accept them, though they didn't really like to. Suddenly his father rose from the bench where they were all sitting.

'You know, I feel rather tired,' said the Professor. 'I was working late on some papers last night – and late nights do me no good at my age. I think I'd better go home to bed!'

'Oh, we'll all come too!' said Aunt Fanny.

'No, no,' the Professor protested. 'I'd hate to spoil the evening's fun for the rest of you.'

'Well, let me drive you back, then,' said Uncle Quentin.

The two scientists got into Uncle Quentin's car – and George and her cousins exchanged surreptitious glances! What a clever excuse the Professor had found for going back to Kirrin Cottage, where he would be alone! It sounded perfectly simple and natural.

Uncle Quentin was soon back. He gave his wife and the children a meaningful look, too. Everything was going just as they'd planned!

The second half of the circus performance began. This time, naturally enough, the Five couldn't take much interest in it (with the exception of Timmy, that is). They were thinking of what must be going on at Kirrin Cottage at that very moment.

There were policemen in hiding inside the house – Uncle Quentin had asked the Inspector to station them where they could see the Professor, and he couldn't see them. So if he did try forcing the safe, thinking he was alone, he'd be caught red handed.

Aunt Fanny and Uncle Quentin did their best to keep their eyes on the circus ring – but the children couldn't help glancing round from time to time, hoping to see the policemen turn up in triumph. And suddenly Julian realised that Alex had noticed they had something on their minds. Alex was looking worried . . . Under cover of the sound of applause, Julian whispered to his brother.

'Better watch out, Dick! Alex suspects something!'

George herself had just noticed the change in Alex's attitude. At that very moment he was looking at Anne, who kept glancing at the tent entrance, and he had a nasty look in his eyes. His jaw was set firm. All of a sudden he didn't look like a nice, smiling lad of seventeen in the least. He looked grown up, and very much on his guard – and dangerous!

Anne was the only one who hadn't noticed the change in the atmosphere. The rest of the children

pulled themselves together and tried to give all their attention to the peformance. Julian thought of a way to try dispelling Alex's suspicions.

'Anne, it's no use looking for the ice cream seller now!' he told his little sister. 'Anyway, you've had quite enough ices already!'

Anne realised she was being called to order – and she knew why! Rather red in the face, she went back to watching the show. Alex seemed to relax.

But now the Five had no doubt about it at all. They *had* been right about the Kolkovs! Professor Kolkov must have been arrested by now – so why didn't the police come to say so and arrest Alex too?

At last the show was over. Aunt Fanny and Uncle Quentin, Alex and the Five all made for the way out of the Big Top. It was a lovely warm night, with a clear sky, and the moon and the stars were shining. The audience dispersed, talking about the show.

Suddenly three men in uniform appeared from behind one of the circus caravans. One of them was Uncle Quentin's friend the Inspector. He came over to the party from Kirrin Cottage.

'Mission accomplished!' he said quietly into Uncle Quentin's ear. 'I thought we'd wait for you outside, rather than make a big fuss of the whole thing. Right, young man – I arrest you in the name of the Law!' he said out loud, turning to Alex.

He signed to the two constables who were with him, and they moved towards Alex to seize him. The children shuddered – so they'd been quite right and the Kolkovs *were* spies. To think how friendly they'd been to Alex! Well, his game was up now.

But the constables hadn't expected the young man to move so quickly. He had already got wind of something suspicious, and now he was sure of it. He shot away, running like a hare, before anyone could do anything about it. He ran round the caravan, jostled past the last of the audience, and made for the dense wood at the side of the field.

'It'll be difficult to catch him if he gets in among those trees!' said Julian.

'Yes,' agreed Dick. 'He's the sort who can look after himself all right! Under cover of night, he'd get a head start – probably make his way to the main road and hitch a lift to London.'

'Or he might steal a ride in a goods train,' suggested Anne, remembering an exciting spy story she had read not long ago. This was just as exciting as the book had been!

Meanwhile the policemen and Uncle Quentin had set off after Alex. Aunt Fanny said she would wait in the car – but if she'd expected the children to follow her example she was wrong. And while her cousins were talking, George herself had been acting. Pointing to the fleeing figure of Alex, she told Timmy, 'Get him, Tim! Good dog! *Get him*!'

Timmy shot off straight away, with just one brief 'Woof!' to show he understood. And he could go faster than Alex, because he had four legs instead of two! George ran after him, of course, and Julian, Dick and Anne ran after *her* – which made four grown-ups, four children and one dog, all in pursuit of Alex.

Unfortunately, the field was a bumpy one, full of treacherous little holes and ruts, with gorse bushes, and clods of earth and stones to trip you up. All this slowed them down. Alex ran so fast you'd have thought he could see all these traps in the dark – but of course he knew only speed could save him. Still, he was no match for Timmy!

'Go on, Timmy!' shouted George, watching her dog's progress. 'Get him!'

And Timmy ran faster than ever when he heard her voice.

Seeing the woods coming closer, Alex made one last effort to reach them. But it was too late! Timmy had reached *him*.

It was all over for the young spy now. He tried to shake the dog off and get free, but Timmy hung on like grim death. When George and the policemen caught up, he was trying to throttle the dog. The three men had quite a struggle to overpower him. At last he was in handcuffs. His jaw was set – he looked furious, and every bit of his real age of twenty-two!

Timmy's eyes were looking slightly glazed – George was making a big fuss of him. She was both triumphant and furious. 'If that brute had strangled you, *I'd* have throttled *him* with my own hands!' she told her dog.

Uncle Quentin, Dick, Julian and Anne arrived in their turn, and they all told brave Timmy what a good dog he'd been. Then they went off back to Kirrin Cottage, where two more police constables were guarding their other prisoner, Professor Kolkov. The Professor was looking even angrier than his son – assuming Alex really was his son!

'Good work!' said the Inspector, when the entire party had gathered in the sitting room of Kirrin Cottage. 'Congratulations, children – you put us on the track of these two nasty pieces of work!' He pointed to the Professor, and told Uncle Quentin, 'This man was actually taking photographs of your plans after forcing the safe to get at them, just as you expected. But we caught him red-handed.'

'*In flagrante delicto*,' said Dick cheerfully – showing off, because he had just found out what it meant, and he kindly told everyone else. 'That's Latin for "caught in the act"!'

'Quite correct!' said the Inspector, laughing. 'Well, now we'll take this precious pair off to the cells and they'll be up in court tomorrow. Of course we'll let you know what happens.'

Uncle Quentin had to be very firm about it before the children would go to bed that evening! They went over the day's events again and again. What an exciting adventure! They felt proud of the Inspector's compliments, and as for Timmy, he was so over-excited that he kept jumping around, and there was no holding him.

Next morning was a bit of an anti-climax. They had nothing to do but wait for news – and it wasn't until early afternoon that Uncle Quentin was summoned to the police station and came back with some!

The children ran to meet him when he came back. 'What's happened?' asked George eagerly.

'Well, thanks to you children, the police have laid hands on two notorious spies! The men they arrested here yesterday are not really Nicholas and Alex Kolkov, just as you guessed. Their real names are Zekov and Rakin. Like the Kolkovs, they do come from a Central European country in the first place, but that's the only likeness. The genuine scientist and his son arrived at London Airport, and we saw them being interviewed on television – but they were kidnapped soon afterwards by an international spy ring. An independent organisation, incidentally.'

'You mean they don't even have the excuse of working on behalf of their own country?' said Julian.

'That's right, my boy,' Uncle Quentin told him. 'The only aim of this spy ring is to get all the money they can by selling any secrets they can lay hands on to the highest bidder!'

'My word – an international spy ring!' repeated Dick, staggered.

'Yes, it calls itself CHECK, referring to the word "checkmate" in the game of chess,' Uncle Quentin said.

'But,' asked George, 'what has happened to the *real* Kolkovs?'

Chapter Six

THE OLD FORT

'The real Kolkovs? After kidnapping them the CHECK organisation hid them in a safe place,' Uncle Quentin told the children. 'They'll be set free any time now.'

'But why did the other two men pretend to be the Kolkovs?' asked Anne.

'You may well ask, my dear!' said Uncle Quentin, smiling at her. 'The idea of the masquerade was to allow the imposters to spy on the scientists at the Trentingham conference, find out all the secrets they could, and get hold of a lot of valuable documents, or else photograph them. Then they were going to sell the secrets and the documents to any country who would pay well for them.'

'All the same, Uncle Quentin, weren't the imposters running awful risks?' asked Dick.

'Pretending to be people as well-known as Professor Kolkov and his son!'

'It wasn't as risky as you might think, Dick,' said his uncle. 'To start with, Zekov and Rakin are either Varanians themselves or come from the little country next to Varania – the police are not sure which. So in any case, they know the country and its language. And then Zekov is a very clever, intelligent man. Playing the part of Nicholas Kolkov was made easier for him because the old scientist is said to be rather gruff in his manner, and not inclined to talk much – and he had all the documents they'd stolen from their victim, the real Professor, of course. He could put up a pretty good show – as we know, since –' And here Uncle Quentin interrupted himself and smiled at the children. 'I was just going to say, since he took us all in! But he didn't take *you* in, did he? If you hadn't noticed his wig and his unpleasant ways when he thought he was on his own, and the fact that his accomplice was a good deal older than seventeen – and if you hadn't kept watch on them, and followed Alex when he came back from the island – if you hadn't suspected him of stealing that document from Trentingham, because you were quite right and he *was* the thief – and if you hadn't handled it all so cleverly, well, the fact is our conference might have ended in real disaster!'

Goodness – what a tribute, coming from Uncle

Quentin!

'Well, all's well that ends well, right?' said Julian, looking pleased.

Uncle Quentin smiled.

'Let's say all *will* be well when it *has* ended well, and the real Kolkov and his son are free again,' he said. 'But that ought to happen any moment now. The police had a hard time of it getting information out of the two spies. They didn't want to say where the Kolkovs were hidden, for fear their accomplices would take revenge on them.'

'But where *did* the spy ring hide the Kolkovs?' asked George, feeling curious.

'Not so very far from here, as it happens. In the old dungeons of Corrie Castle – they've been closed to the public for a long time now, because of crumbling masonry. The Inspector said he'd telephone me as soon as they'd found Professor Kolkov and his son.'

'Why have they waited so long?' asked Anne in surprise.

'Because it took quite a while to get the name of the hiding place out of Zekov and Rakin, as I told you, and then the police had to organise the operation carefully, so as not to endanger the captives themselves during the rescue attempt.'

'I don't think I'll feel quite happy about it until we know the old Professor and his son are safe and sound, though,' said Anne. She still sounded worried.

Just then the telephone rang.

'Ah, that'll be the Inspector now!' said Uncle Quentin. 'He must be ringing to tell me everything's all right, and then I can go and fetch the Kolkovs and bring them back here. They'll need a good rest! Hallo? Yes . . . yes . . .'

His smile suddenly disappeared. The children saw him frown.

'There's something wrong!' Julian whispered.

'What?' said Uncle Quentin. 'You *haven't* got the Kolkovs? Nobody in the ruined castle at all? Yes . . . I see . . . yes, my own opinion entirely, Inspector. The CHECK spy ring must have heard you'd arrested Zekov and Rakin, and they immediately moved their prisoners to another hiding place. Dear, dear . . . yes, I'm very sorry about all this . . . yes, please ring me back the moment you have any information.'

And he put the receiver down. He had no need to explain anything. George and her cousins had realised what was up from his side of the conversation.

'Oh, what bad luck!' said Dick. 'The poor Kolkovs! But why does CHECK want to keep them now that the whole plot's been discovered?'

'Perhaps they want to try getting more secrets out of the real Professor?' Anne suggested.

'Or they're planning to use them as hostages,'

said George. 'Perhaps they hope to swap them for the two imposters!'

'I've no more idea about it than you children have, I'm afraid,' said Uncle Quentin – and he went to find Aunt Fanny and tell *her* the latest news too.

Left on their own, the Five looked at each other in silence.

'We can't let a thing like this happen!' growled George, quite angrily.

'Those poor, *poor* people!' wailed Anne, with her eyes full of tears.

'Oh, for goodness' sake don't be a cry-baby, Anne!' said her cousin. 'It's no good weeping and wailing – we must *do* something!'

'Yes, but what?' asked Julian gloomily.

'We could go to Corrie Castle for a start, and search the ruins ourselves,' said George.

'Good idea!' said Dick, guessing what was in his cousin's mind. 'We might find some clue to put us on the track of the missing Kolkovs.'

'It's not very likely,' said Julian, shaking his head. 'You don't suppose the police didn't search the place thoroughly, do you?'

'No, of course they'll have made a good search,' said George. 'But they were really looking for two men, and they didn't find them. There might have been small clues they missed – just tiny details.'

'Well, it certainly won't do any harm to go for a

bicycle ride to the castle and take a look,' Julian agreed.

'Woof!' said Timmy firmly, seeing the children making for the door. That meant a walk – and a walk meant chasing rabbits!

The Five set off straight away. They had several hours' free time before supper, so there was no great hurry, and they cycled along at a leisurely pace. They had thought of bringing powerful torches with them, to help them search the dungeons of Corrie Castle.

They found the ruins deserted. The police operation had been such a quiet and professional one that the general public didn't even know about it, and there were no idle sightseers standing about and gaping.

'Well, that suits us!' said George. 'Come on, let's start searching!'

She left her bicycle in the bushes and slipped under the barbed wire surrounding the castle ruins. Her cousins followed her.

Soon the Five were cautiously making their way down into the dungeons. They were very solidly built, made to last for centuries – it was the ruins above ground that made it rather dangerous to go down there. But the Five took great care.

They found that three of the dungeons had obviously been used quite recently. There were leaves and branches put down on the floors to make beds of a kind, and the remains of a meal. But if they had contained anything else interesting, then the police had taken it away.

'This one must have been occupied by the man guarding the two prisoners,' said Julian. 'It has no lock on the door.'

'No – and the other two have brand new bolts on the outsides!' Dick noticed. 'So that's where Professor Kolkov and his son were kept prisoner.'

The dungeon Julian had looked inside still contained a newspaper and an empty cigarette packet. There was nothing except the makeshift beds left in the other two.

'I expect the police will take those branches away tomorrow,' said Anne. She felt quite upset to be looking at a place where the two poor prisoners had been kept so recently.

'Hallo!' said George suddenly, seeing Timmy rummaging around in a corner. 'Have you found something, old fellow?'

'Woof!' barked Timmy happily.

And he flicked something up in the air with his paw, just as if he were playing with it. George caught it before it fell to the ground. It was a little ball of something white.

'I say – it's a crumpled-up handkerchief,' said George. She was smoothing it out as she spoke, and suddenly her cousins heard her let out a yell of triumph.

'And it's got something written on it,' she cried. 'A message in English, signed Alex Kolkov!'

'My word – let's have a look – read it out, George – woof!' said everyone else all at once. George spread the handkerchief out on her knee and managed to decipher the message: not a very easy task, since it had been written on the white cotton with a ballpoint pen which had smudged.

'To anyone who might be able to help – my father Nicholas Kolkov and I are prisoners of an international spy ring called CHECK –'

'We know that already!' said Anne.

'Yes, but he doesn't know we know, does he, you silly thing?' said George. 'He doesn't even know who's looking for him. Now, listen to the rest of it.' And she went on reading. 'I don't know just where we are now, but this morning I heard two men talk of moving us to another prison which one of them called *the old fort*. This may be a useful clue. Signed: Alex Kolkov.'

'The old fort?' cried Dick excitedly. 'Why – that must be –'

'The old fort which stands above the beach near Winkle Bay!' finished Julian. 'Remember how we played hide-and-seek there last summer?'

'Yes, that must be where they've taken the Kolkovs all right!' agreed George. 'Somebody bought the ruins of the fort recently – they're going to be allowed to knock them down, because they're not really of any great historical interest, and build a new hotel there instead. But the demolition and building isn't to start until the autumn, although the public's not allowed in any more. Not many people ever went there anyway – the place is full of grass snakes. Perfectly harmless, but some people are scared of them.'

'*I* am, for one!' Anne admitted. 'That's why we stopped going there to play!'

Julian was frowning thoughtfully. 'I think the best thing to do is take this message straight to the police,' he said. 'They'll know what steps to take next.'

But Dick and George both looked at him quite scornfully!

'Honestly, Ju, what a feeble idea!' cried George. 'We've got on the prisoners' trail, haven't we? We don't want them disappearing from under our very noses for a *second* time!'

'Hear, hear!' Dick agreed. 'Listen, Julian – the spies will be on the alert now, won't they? And they're sure to notice if they see a lot of policemen roaming about! If they take fright and move the Kolkovs *again*, in a hurry as they did before, we can't rely on Alex being able to leave another clue behind him!'

But Julian still wasn't convinced.

'I imagine the spies are only using the old fort above Winkle Bay as a temporary hiding place,' he pointed out. 'As soon as they've all had time to consult each other, they'll move their prisoners somewhere else, much farther off!'

'No, they won't!' George contradicted him. 'Or not very easily. Didn't you hear the news on the radio? The newsreader said all roads were being watched, and there were road blocks up, and all sorts of other things to stop the spies getting away!'

'You know, Julian, I think George and Dick are right,' said little Anne, rather timidly, because usually she agreed with everything her big brother said. She admired him so much! But for once she was on the side of the other two. 'The kidnappers are more or less stuck in this part of the country, aren't they? They've *got* to go to ground and stay there!'

'Quite right, Anne!' said Dick. 'However, we want to act to free the two Kolkovs as fast as we can.'

In the end Julian let the others persuade him to agree with them. And once he *had* been won over, he was the one who came up with the best idea for a way to get near the fort without arousing the spies' suspicions.

'I know what we can do,' he said. 'We'll pretend to be campers just passing through this part of the country. We can put our tents up in the meadow outside the fort. Then all our comings and goings will look perfectly natural – and we can keep watch.

on the place without seeming to!'

'Oh, but what about the snakes?' asked Anne, anxiously. 'Suppose there are vipers?'

'Well, there aren't! Only grass snakes – I told you so, last year!' said George. 'Grass snakes are bigger, but they're not at all dangerous.'

'And you could always try cooking them, Anne, like eels!' suggested Dick, teasing his little sister. 'I tell you what – I'll catch you some, and you can cook them for our supper!'

Poor Anne! She squealed with horror, and Julian and George couldn't help laughing. Timmy barked. A hearty laugh did all the children good, and they stopped arguing. Now all they had to do was put their plan into practice.

There wasn't any difficulty at home when they said they'd like to go and camp outside the old fort. Aunt Fanny and Uncle Quentin thought fresh air was good for children, and they gave their permission at once. Aunt Fanny went to the larder and found some food for the Five to take with them. And next day they set off with two lightweight trailers hitched to the boys' bicycles. The trailers were packed with their tents, sleeping bags, provisions and all the other things you'd need to go camping for several days.

Timmy sat enthroned in George's bicycle basket with his ears streaming in the wind. He looked a bit like a Roman emperor in a triumphal chariot!

The old fort was about twelve kilometres from Kirrin Cottage, along a stony little road which rose in a steep slope. It was a hot day, and the four children found they were perspiring freely as they cycled along.

'Keep going, everyone!' panted Dick. 'There's a refreshment room at the top of the hill!'

'Is there really?' asked Anne, who thought he meant it.

'Yes, of course – a nice little spring of water where the grass snakes come to drink!' her brother teased her.

'Oh, shut up, Dick!' said George. 'You'd better keep your breath for getting up this last slope. And everyone remember what we're going to do when we reach the top.'

'Don't worry,' said Julian. 'We'll all talk very loud about making our camp and settling in, so that anyone hearing us will think we're just harmless tourists.'

'Maybe we ought to try and think of some way to let the Kolkovs know *we* know they're in the fort, and we hope to get them out,' Dick suggested.

'That's all right, Dick,' George told hm. 'I've thought of everything!'

Then Julian suddenly stopped cycling, and got off his bike, signalling to the others to copy him. They did, although they were rather surprised.

'What's the matter?' asked Dick. '*You're* not

usually the first to get off your bike going uphill, Ju! Come on – it's not much farther now!'

'It's nothing to do with that,' said Julian. 'I was thinking of something you said just now.'

'What was it?' asked Dick, who had already forgotten.

'About hoping to get the prisoners out! We've been in such a hurry to get to the Kolkovs, we haven't stopped to think of any way to rescue them!'

'Oh, we'll think up a way when we get there,' said George impatiently. 'And if we really can't think of one, *then* we'll call the police in! Just now the main thing is to make sure the Kolkovs really are up there – so come on, everyone!'

And they all cycled on again. Timmy had been stretching his legs while they stopped to talk, chasing about in search of rabbits. Now he ran on ahead of the rest of the party, barking happily at the trees and the butterflies.

George and her cousins reached the top of the path and the big meadow where the old fort stood. They began talking and shouting in very loud voices, so as to give any spies who might be eavesdropping plenty of information about themselves – misleading information, of course!

'Great!' cried Julian. 'Here's a fine place to put the tents up!'

'Oh, don't let's go too near the fort!' said Anne.

'I know it's full of snakes, and I'm so scared of snaky things!'

'Don't worry, we're not a bit interested in that old fort!' George assured her cousin at the top of her voice. She was standing beside a little stream. 'Come over here, all of you! This is a good place – trees for shelter, and a stream to give us water!'

'You're right,' Dick shouted back. 'This is our camping place! Come along, hurry up, everyone!'

So Julian, Dick and Anne hurried over to join George and Timmy. Making out that they were simply delighted by the wonderful view of the countryside they had from the hill-top, the Five turned their backs on the fort to look out at the sea below them. Then, once their enthusiasm seemed to be dying down a bit, they started unpacking all their camping things.

'I feel just as if there were eyes watching us,' Anne whispered to her cousin.

'Let's hope there *are*!' George whispered back.' 'That would mean the enemy are really there – along with their prisoners!'

The boys put the tents up in a noisy, showy sort of way. Meanwhile George had to cope with an unexpected problem. Timmy stopped chasing butterflies and decided he would like to go and explore the old fort instead. He put his nose to the ground and picked up what was obviously an interesting scent – and he growled when George

caught him by the scruff of his neck and made him come back to the stream.

She put her face close to his and talked to him in a low voice for several minutes.

'Now, do you get that?' she finished. 'You just be a good dog and stay with me! No roaming off, understand?'

Timmy was rather surprised – George usually let him go where he liked, so long as he wasn't a nuisance. All the same, he showed that he *did* understand. 'Woof!' he said, rather sadly.

Then he resigned himself to trotting along in George's wake.

Anne was building a barbecue – and trying to think of a way to let the prisoners know there were friends near at hand! That would cheer them, and it would mean they'd be ready when rescue came. But unfortunately the little girl couldn't think of anything clever just at the moment.

It was a cheerful meal. Anyone watching the children would have sworn they hadn't a care in the world! And they really *did* enjoy the sausages Anne had grilled on her barbecue, and drank lots of lemonade – all that shouting at each other had made them thirsty. However, they kept their eyes open all the time. But there was no sign of life from the fort. And no noise, either. Julian was beginning to wonder gloomily if this really *was* the 'old fort' Alex Kolkov's jailers had mentioned after all.

After their meal the Five had a game of ball. This helped them to get closer to the old building without looking as if they were much interested in it. George had reminded Timmy not to go sniffing about among the ruins.

But it was no use! The children practically wore themselves out rushing up and down, casting furtive glances at the old walls, but they saw nothing at all suspicious. So they spent the rest of the day making their camp nice and comfortable.

When dark fell they gathered round the camp-fire and Dick took out his mouth organ. Anne began humming a tune. Julian was whittling a piece of wood with his knife. George was sitting cross-legged, automatically patting Timmy, who lay beside her. She could see the old fort across the meadow if she looked over Dick's shoulder. And suddenly she stiffened.

'Dick!' she breathed. 'Go on playing. The rest of you don't look at the fort. Don't look as if you're doing anything much! I've just seen something move. *Someone*, rather! Yes – yes, it's a funny shape coming out of the entrance!'

Chapter Seven

THE REAL ALEX

'Ssh, Timmy! Keep still!' George whispered to her dog.

'What exactly does it look like?' asked Julian in an undertone.

'The shape? It's like somebody riding a horse – no! No, it's someone on a motor-bike. He's kicking it along with his feet, not using the engine.'

'So as not to be heard, of course!'

'I can hardly see him – he's starting down the hill,' said George.

'One of the Kolkovs' jailers!' whispered Anne, very excited. 'So this fort *is* the right one after all!'

Dick had stopped playing. None of the children moved a muscle, but they were all straining their ears. It seemed ages before they heard a distant roar and rattle.

'Our man waited to get down to the main road

before he switched his engine on!' said Julian.

'I wonder where he's going?' asked Anne in a low voice.

'To get in touch with his accomplices, I expect,' said Dick. 'And tell them we're here, and ask what to do! Or else he's just off to stock up with provisions, or find out what the news is!'

'I wish I knew if there was more than one jailer guarding the prisoners,' said George thoughtfully. 'If the man we've just seen was the *only* guard, we could go and try exploring the fort now. But I suppose there must be at least two. One man on his own couldn't have brought the Kolkovs here.'

The children decided to be on the safe side, and went into their tents – but they didn't go to sleep. They were all listening for the motor-bike to come back.

At last they heard the faint sound of an engine, and they all pricked up their ears. They could see through the tent openings. The engine was switched off all of a sudden, and a moment later a silent shadow appeared at the top of the slope, pushing the motor-bike.

At the very same moment, an equally silent shadow emerged from the ruins.

'There!' George whispered to Anne. 'There *are* two of them!'

The new arrival said something to his accomplice in a low voice, and then they both disappeared inside the fort. Obviously the Five couldn't hope to see or hear any more this evening! And so they went to sleep, feeling quite tired.

Anne was very cheerful when she got up next morning. A bright idea had come to her overnight – she'd thought of a clever way to get in touch with the prisoners.

As she made breakfast, she told her brothers and George about it.

'You see, we've simply got to let the Kolkovs know *we* know they're in the fort, and there's help coming,' she explained.

'And *they* might think about trying to let *us* know they're there,' grumbled Dick. He was getting rather tired of waiting about.

'That's quite a different problem,' George interrupted him impatiently. 'Let Anne finish what she was saying!'

'Well, I think I've thought of a way,' Anne went on modestly. 'I'll go and pick flowers near the fort, and while I'm picking them I'll sing.'

'And then what?' asked Julian. He couldn't see what his little sister was getting at.

'I'll change the words of the song round, you see, so that the prisoners will realise something's happened!' Anne told him.

'And so will their jailers!' said George, smiling.

'No, they won't! Let me explain. I'll mention something only the Kolkovs know about, and *not* their kidnappers!'

'Oh yes, I see!' said George. 'The handkerchief rolled up into a ball, with Alex's message on it!'

'That's right,' Anne told her. 'Alex will know somebody's found the handkerchief and read the message – and he'll know we know he and his father are here, too.'

'And so he'll deduce that there's a rescue coming!' Julian finished. 'Well done, Anne – jolly good idea!'

The children finished their breakfast quickly, and Julian, Dick and George said they would clear away and wash up, while Anne went off in the direction of the fort, humming to herself.

When she got close to the old walls, the little girl began picking the wild flowers that grew near the fort – buttercups and ox-eye daisies. Some of them grew on the walls themselves. And she sang louder than before. The words of her song went like this:

'I sent a hanky to my love,
And on the way I dropped it!
A little girl has picked it up
And put it in her pocket.'

She sang the little verse several times over as she wandered round the outside of the fort, picking flowers. It really was a clever idea! What could look more innocent than a pretty little fair-haired girl singing a nursery rhyme and picking wild flowers out in the meadows? She told herself that if the spies did hear what she was singing, they wouldn't be likely to know that she wasn't following the exact words of the nursery rhyme – and even if they did, she'd said nothing to give herself away. They might not like seeing somebody so close to the fort, but they couldn't come out and tell her to go away for fear of betraying their own presence!

She was just singing the verse for the eighth time in her clear little voice when she thought she heard a faint whistle almost at her feet. The first thing she thought of was snakes, and she shivered. She hated them so much, even grass snakes! But it wasn't a snake after all.

Looking round, she saw a barred cellar window just showing above ground level. And another soft whistle came from it!

Still humming and picking flowers, Anne made her way over to the cellar window and looked through the bars.

There wasn't any glass in the window. At first all she could see was a dark hole. Then, as her eyes got used to the dim light, she made out two human figures lying on thin mattresses. So far as she could make out, they were tied up.

Anne's heart was in her mouth! She was quite sure she had found the two real Kolkovs!

One of the figures, the smaller one, managed to crawl over the floor somehow until he was close to

the window. She saw a pale face looking up at her. It belonged to a fair-haired boy of about seventeen!

'Miss – so you found my handkerchief?' he whispered.

Anne crouched down to the bars of the window. 'Oh – you *are* Alex Kolkov, aren't you?' she whispered.

'Yes – keep your voice down! Our guards mustn't suspect anything! They've tied us up, but they didn't gag us!'

'Why not? You could have called for help!'

Alex smiled at her sadly. 'Yes – and they threatened to keep us permanently gagged if we thought of doing anything of the kind! One squeak out of us, they said, and they'd make sure we were sorry for it. Anyway, what hope was there of being heard and rescued in a secluded place like this?'

'Well, don't worry!' Anne told him. 'We're here – my brothers and my cousin George. She's Quentin Kirrin's daughter, and you were coming to stay with us at Kirrin Cottage. We're going to help you, but we couldn't do anything until we knew where they were keeping you. Well, now we do – and you won't have much longer to wait! So cheer up! I'd better not linger here any more.'

And she rose to her feet and went on picking flowers, looking casual, but moving gradually away from the fort this time. She was back with the other children not long afterwards.

'What happened?' asked Dick at once. 'You were ages! We thought you were *never* coming back. Well – did you see anything?'

'Oh yes – yes, I did! I've found the Kolkovs!' Anne told them.

Her news was a real bombshell.

'Anne – that's marvellous!' cried George. 'We know for certain at last!'

'Ssh! Calm down!' said Julian. 'You don't want those spies to get suspicious of us now, do you?'

But it wasn't easy for George to calm down. 'Quick – let's draw up a plan of attack straight away!' she said.

'Plan of attack? *Rescue* plan is what you mean!' said Julian. 'You're not seriously thinking of tackling an international spy ring head on, are you?'

'No, of course not,' George agreed. She could be quite sensible at times! 'What we've got to do is set the two prisoners free with as little fuss as possible, and then go to the police once they're in safety, and the police can pick up their kidnappers!'

But Julian still shook his head. 'That's no use either, George. The best thing to do is go back to Kirrin Cottage straight away, tell Uncle Quentin, and get him to tell the police.'

'And the police will arrive to find their birds flown!' Dick pointed out. 'That's a dead cert!'

'Hear, hear!' George agreed. 'It would be only too easy for the police to give themselves away before they even started the operation – and then the spies would have advance warning, and plenty of time to run for it! Taking their hostages with them! Remember what happened at Corrie Castle, Ju? Well, it could easily happen again, so don't be so slow and stuffy! Help us think how to rescue the Kolkovs instead!'

'Oh, all right!' said Julian. 'But we must plan everything very carefully.'

As the children didn't want to run the slightest risk of being overheard, if one of the spies happened to venture out of the fort, they decided to get well away from their camping place to hold a council of war.

Dick had a good idea. 'Let's go down to the beach in the bay!' he suggested. 'Nobody can hear us there, and if anyone comes along we'll easily be able to see them!'

'All right,' Julian agreed. 'We can take this little path – it goes right down to the shingle.'

The shingle in Winkle Bay wasn't nearly as comfortable as the nice yellow sand on the beach at Kirrin – but it was a long way from anywhere, and that was what mattered.

'Keep watch, Timmy!' George told her dog. 'Good boy! Bark if you see anyone coming!'

Timmy took himself very seriously as a watchdog. He sat down with his nose in the air and his ears pricked up, ready to pick up any strange sight, scent or sound.

The four cousins all looked at each other. 'Now then,' Julian began, 'we've got to get this right first time, because we won't be likely to have a second chance if we put a foot wrong. So we must plan it all out in detail – though I *still* think –'

'Oh no – you're not going to start on like that again, are you?' groaned George. 'I know we're taking on a lot, but we've made our minds up, so come on and think how to do it!'

'All right, all right, we're going to set the Kolkovs free with our own fair hands!' laughed Dick. 'The only question is, how?'

'Well, there aren't all that many ways of doing it!' said George. 'We have to get them out of that cellar they're in. We'll need files to file through the bars, and ropes to haul the prisoners up.'

'You're forgetting their guards, aren't you?' said Dick.

'We'll keep so quiet they won't hear us.'

'And you're forgetting something else,' Julian reminded his cousin. 'The Kolkovs are tied up.'

'But not too tightly,' said Anne. 'Alex was just able to crawl over to the window and talk to me, if he twisted about a bit.'

'All the same, it would be better if they could move freely before we try hoisting them out,'

Julian said. 'I wonder if they could manage to cut their own bonds if we passed a knife in through the bars? An open penknife! That would give them time to get some feeling back in their legs and arms while we file through the bars – they must be awfully numb if they've been tied up all this time.'

Anne agreed with her big brother.

'They might even be able to help file through the bars themselves,' she pointed out. 'They didn't look to me very thick bars – and I think they're rusty, too.'

'Right. I'll pass them a knife,' said George. 'And Dick and I have got our lassoes with us!'

A little while ago the two cousins had had a lasso craze! They had got very clever at throwing their ropes, and now they took them everywhere – you never knew when a lasso might come in useful!

'What about files, though?' said Dick. 'We haven't got any files!'

'We can always buy some, you ass!' Julian pointed out. 'Or proper saws for cutting metal. I'll go and see what I can get.'

'And I'll come too!' said Anne. 'If they're watching us from the fort, they'll think we're off for a bicycle ride, or going to stock up with provisions.'

'And I'll keep watch on the fort while you're gone,' said Dick.

'I'll see about getting a knife in to Alex, with a note explaining what we want him and his father to do,' said George.

'When do we start?' asked Anne.

'Tonight, of course,' said her cousin. 'The sooner we can rescue the Kolkovs the better!'

Now they had made their plans, the Five felt it was safe to go back up the cliff, and soon they were in their camp again. The boys and George helped Anne to make a quick lunch of baked beans and beefburgers, and while they ate it Dick turned on his little radio to hear the news. Suddenly the Five pricked up their ears! The newsreader had come to a very interesting item.

'Here is the latest news of the Trentingham kidnapping. Professor Kolkov and his son are still missing, but CHECK, the sinister organisation responsible for abducting them, has got in touch with the authorities . . .'

'Golly!' said George. The children listened harder than ever.

'According to CHECK, their prisoners have been flown to a foreign country in a private aircraft –'

'What a lie!' said Anne indignantly.

'Ssh!' hissed George. 'We must listen to this.'

'The kidnappers have given the police an ultimatum. CHECK will exchange the Kolkovs for the two members of their own organisation who attended the Trentingham conference instead of the Professor and his son, the men known as Zekov and Rakin, top-ranking spies who are now being held in custody. No reply has yet been given to the kidnappers.'

'You see?' cried George. 'We *must* rescue the Kolkovs – it's more urgent than ever now! If the exchange does take place those two wicked imposters will get away scot free, and start spying for CHECK again!'

'What's more, if the police turn the ultimatum down, Alex and his father will be in great danger!' said Dick.

Julian was already on his feet.

'So let's not waste any more time!' he said. 'I'm off to the nearest town to buy some files.'

'And I'll sharpen the blade for the penknife I'm going to pass in to the Kolkovs,' said George. 'It must have a really good edge on it, because they'll have difficulty cutting their bonds at all with their hands tied.'

'They'll need one of them to hold the knife as firmly as possible while the other rubs the rope tying his hands against the blade,' Dick pointed out. 'It may take a bit of time, but it'll work all right.'

'Oh,' said Anne, sighing. 'I do hope so! I do hope *everything* will turn out all right in the end!'

Chapter Eight

PREPARING A RESCUE

Julian and Anne were soon off on their bicycles. Dick made sure the two lassoes were in good condition, while George sharpened her knife. When she had done the job, she wrapped the knife in a piece of paper. She had written her message on the paper in letters large enough to be read in the dim light of the cellar. It ran:

'Try to cut through your bonds this evening after your jailers visit you for the last time today. We plan to rescue you tonight, Be ready!

George Kirrin and her cousins.'

She put a rubber band round the little package.

'Now I'm going for a little stroll near the fort,' she said. 'I'll pass close to the cellar window and drop the knife through the bars as I go by. I won't stop, and I'll be back as soon as I've done it. Even if the spies do spot me they won't suspect anything – I'll just look as if I'm taking Timmy for a walk. Come on, Tim, old chap! Timmy! Where are you?'

Much to her surprise, George realised that her dog had left her side for once!

'Where on earth is he?' she wondered.

Then she and Dick heard barking. Timmy was standing on the edge of a little pond about a hundred metres off, barking at something they couldn't see.

'What's he found this time?' asked Dick.

'No idea! Let's find out,' said George.

They both hurried towards the pond. Timmy saw them coming. He looked at them. 'Woof!' he complained, in a melancholy tone.

'What *are* you up to, Timmy?' asked George.

Timmy began his furious barking again. And the two cousins roared with laughter when they saw a small green frog sitting peacefully on a big stone in the middle of the pond! It looked as if it was making fun of the dog.

At first, Timmy had only wanted to have a game, and he'd invited the frog to play with a very polite little 'Woof?' But obviously the frog didn't trust a big, hairy dog like Timmy! It sat on its stone and wouldn't move. Then Timmy lost his temper and said a lot of rude things about frogs in dog language. The frog didn't seem to mind. Timmy was sure his kind mistress would come and back him up, so he barked harder than ever.'

'Woof! Woof! Woof! Woof, woof!'

'Croak!' went the frog, staring at him with its round, bulging eyes.

George burst out laughing again, and so did Dick.

'Honestly, the frog looks as if it's laughing too, with that great wide mouth!' he said. 'Laughing at poor Timmy!'

'I wouldn't be surprised if that's exactly what it *is* doing!' said George. 'Animals have more of a sense of humour than you might think! Come on, Timmy, old boy. Leave that frog alone and come for a walk with me!'

But Timmy didn't seem to think much of that idea. He was getting really cross with the frog and the way it ignored his invitation. He couldn't get near it himself, either. It was infuriating! Taking no notice of George, he went up to the very edge of the water and let out some more frantic barks.

The frog replied with a tremendous 'Croak!' – and jumped off its stone, to land on Timmy's nose! He was taken completely by surprise. He lost his balance, and fell into the pond.

Trying to find a firm footing and get out again, he slipped even farther in, and almost entirely disappeared. There was nothing of him showing above water but his nose.

This frog evidently *had* got a sense of humour! It

sat on the very tip of that moist, dark nose!

Timmy came up again, and the frog jumped off him and on to the bank. Timmy spat out some water, splashed out with his paws, got back on the bank, shook himself, and then found himself face to face with the frog again! It was rolling its eyes, as if to say, 'Catch me if you can!'

The two cousins were bent over with laughter. For the moment they had quite forgotten about the spies, their prisoners and the sinister CHECK organisation. Their gales of laughter at the sight of Timmy and the frog were giving them a stitch in the side – there was dear old Timmy, covered with mud and looking very fierce, facing his tiny, cheeky adversary.

In between peals of laughter, George managed to gasp, 'Come on, Timmy! Leave the poor thing alone! It hasn't hurt you!'

By now, however, Timmy was as annoyed at being laughed at as by the way the frog was defying him!

The frog batted its heavy eyelids. 'Croak!' it said again. And then it turned its back on the pond and the dog, took a tremendous jump, and disappeared into the long grass. Timmy was furious! He set off after it, but it was no use. The frog could easily escape him, hiding among tufts of grass, jumping one way and then another exactly when Timmy thought he was about to catch it. George was still laughing, but she was afraid Timmy might end up hurting the little creature without meaning to, so she set off after him, and Dick followed *her*.

This frantic chase went on for quite a time. Timmy was beside himself with fury, and the children were gasping with laughter. The only calm one was the frog! It jumped, zigzag fashion, right across the meadow – and it was getting closer and closer to the fort!

Soon it was jumping through the grass by the old walls. At last it jumped up on a stone in the sunlight, right in front of the cellar window which Anne had pointed out as the window of the Kolkovs' prison.

'I say!' George murmured. 'Here's our chance!'

And she ran on – straight towards the window.

It was all over in a few seconds. The frog took another jump just as Timmy thought he was finally going to catch it. George lunged forward to catch her dog by his collar – and as she did so she dropped the knife in through the bars of the window. What luck she had been carrying it on her, carefully wrapped in her note of explanation!

She didn't even stop properly before turning to drag Timmy away, scolding him at the top of her voice.

'Oh, you naughty dog! I *told* you not to come up to the fort. There are lots of snakes here – don't you realise they might have bitten you?'

She ran straight back to the camp, with Dick after her, and both children dropped on the grass, with Timmy in between them.

'Phew!' breathed George. 'Done it! The Kolkovs have got my knife – thanks to Timmy's frog!'

Then she looked at Timmy, and burst out laughing again. Dick joined in. Poor Timmy! He was a very strange sight, covered in mud from head to tail, from the tips of his ears to the end of his paws. The mud made a kind of crust all over him, and it was already drying in the blazing summer sun. His coat stuck out in stiff tufts. He looked like some sort of strange prehistoric monster.

'You can't stay like that, old fellow!' George told him. 'You're going to have a bath!'

Timmy looked very miserable. Having a bath wasn't his favourite way of spending his time at all!

Dick and George heated some water and gave him a good wash. Luckily they had some shampoo with them, and soon Timmy was covered with sweet-smelling lather. He looked very crestfallen. He certainly wasn't going to chase any more frogs if this was what it led to!

Julian and Anne got back quite late in the afternoon. Grumbling rather, because she hated doing anything like housework, George had started making an evening meal, since Anne wasn't there to tackle the job as usual. She was very glad to see her two cousins.

'Well?' all four children asked each other at the same moment.

'I've got a knife in to the Kolkovs,' George told Anne and Julian.

'And we've got some metal files,' said Julian. 'Look!'

'No – don't get them out here,' said Dick quickly. 'Show us in the tent! For all we know, someone's keeping watch on us from the fort through field glasses. We must be extra careful, in full view of the enemy like this!'

'Yes, you're right,' Julian agreed. They went into the tent, and he produced two little files which he had bought in an ironmonger's in the nearest town.

'Only two?' asked George in surprise.

'The cellar window isn't very big,' Julian said. 'There's only room for two people to use the files at once – three would get in each other's way.'

'Yes, you've got a point there,' George admitted. 'Come to think of it, we'll have to find some way of muffling the sound of the file biting into metal!'

'I *have* thought of it!' Julian told her. 'We can wrap towels round the bars – that will muffle the vibrations.'

'Let's hope it works,' said Anne. She was beginning to feel a bit scared. 'Are you sure we'll manage to file through the bars?'

'You said they were pretty rusty yourself,' Julian reminded her.

'Yes, I know. Just so long as the spies don't catch us in the act!'

'Anne,' George told her solemnly, 'don't I *keep* saying "nothing ventured, nothing gained"? Well, it's perfectly true. The game's worth the candle!'

'And the end justifies the means, and we'll see what we will see, and any amount of other proverbs too!' said Dick, laughing at his cousin.

George threw him a playful punch. Timmy barked, Dick ran off and George went after him! Julian and Anne ran too. They all felt they needed to relax a bit. Their game lasted about ten minutes, and by the end of it they were all feeling more hopeful again. Unfortunately, the chops George had put on the barbecue had all shrivelled up – but they took that philosophically, and opened some tins for their supper. Timmy got the dried-out, burnt chops!

'An ill wind that blows nobody good,' murmured Dick, looking at him.

'Oh no – you're not going to start *that* again, are you?' said George, pretending to be cross. 'Dry up, do!'

'And the drying up is just what he *is* going to do!' said Anne, laughing. 'Here, Dick – here's a tea-cloth! I'll wash and you can dry.'

They packed all the picnic things up in their box

again, and then there was nothing to do but wait for nightfall. That was when the Five had decided they must mount their rescue attempt.

To pass the time, they went down to the sea for a bathe. However, they took turns, because you couldn't see the fort from the beach. So while two of the cousins went for a lovely swim, the other two stayed up at their camp, pretending to tidy the place up or play cards, but really keeping an eye on the old building the whole time. There wasn't very much risk they'd fail to notice if the Kolkovs were moved from their hiding place yet again, but they wanted to make quite sure.

At long last night fell, and it got dark. The children carefully put out the camp fire and went into their tents, with Timmy.

Of course they didn't go to bed. They were very much on the alert.

Over in the fort, nothing seemed to be moving. It was a warm, still night. The moon was playing hide-and-seek with drifting clouds, which was a nuisance. The Five needed a long, dark period for their rescue operation.

At last midnight came. This was the time they thought it would be best to act. Keeping very, very quiet, they stole out of their tents and made for the cellar window in the old fort, bending low so that they wouldn't stand out against the sky. Timmy followed them.

Luckily the moon had disappeared behind the clouds at last. But George was worried, all the same. Had the Kolkovs managed to cut themselves free? Had the spies suddenly decided to put them somewhere different? If so they'd have to begin all over again.

At last the little party reached the cellar window, in silence. George put her face to the bars and whispered into the dark. 'Professor Kolkov? Alex? Are you there? It's me, George Kirrin. I slipped you a knife earlier on.'

A young man's voice replied, very quietly and quite close to her.

'Yes – and thank you, Miss Kirrin! My father and I are here, and we've managed to cut the ropes they'd used to tie us up.'

'Good!' said George happily. 'Now, my cousins and I are going to file through these bars. We've got the tools we need for that!'

'Oh, could you give me one, please?' asked Alex. 'It's only right *I* should do something to help!'

'Please be quick, Miss Kirrin – and thank you, with all my heart!' said another voice inside the cellar. Professor Kolkov, of course – the real Professor Kolkov this time.

The Five and the two Kolkovs soon got organised. Anne and George kept watch, with Timmy to help them, while Julian filed at the bars from outside the window and Alex filed from the inside. They tackled a bar each. They had wrapped towels round the bars, as Julian had suggested, but though that did reduce the noise of the vibrating metal, you could still hear it.

When Julian and Alex got tired, Dick and Professor Kolkov took over.

Unfortunately the work didn't go as fast as the children had hoped. The files weren't very good quality, and didn't bite into the bars very well. And none of the four using them was used to this sort of work. What was more, the Kolkovs, standing on an old crate down in the cellar, still had to reach up to get at the window, and so they soon got tired. Time seemed to be passing very slowly.

George was seething with impatience. She started wondering if they would *ever* manage to cut through those bars. Surely somebody would hear them eventually! As for Anne, she didn't know just why, but she felt badly worried. Timmy was keeping quite still. He might have been a stone statue of a dog. Only his alert look and the way he pricked his ears up showed that he was wide awake and on the watch.

Suddenly he raised his head, gave a low growl, and looked round. At that very moment there was a loud noise inside the cellar, and a bright light went on! Startled and alarmed, Dick and Julian were able to see the inside of the prison cell.

Two men were standing there. They had just opened the door – and they were training pistols on the two Kolkovs.

Chapter Nine

A FINAL SHOWDOWN

'Don't any of you move!' one of them ordered. 'Now – tie those two up again, and hurry up about it!'

The other man put his pistol in his holster and set about tying the Kolkovs up. Poor things, they were completely taken by surprise, and couldn't put up any resistance – the other man's pistol was pointing at them.

Julian pulled himself together. He jumped up, shouting, 'Run for it, everyone!'

But it was too late. As Julian, Dick, George and Anne got ready to take off into the night, two more men emerged from the shadows and barred their way.

'Oh no! There are *more* than two of them!' groaned George.

'There are four of us, young man!' said one of the

newcomers jovially, and in a slight foreign accent. Like so many other people, he thought George really was a boy. That sort of mistake usually amused her, but she couldn't find anything funny in it tonight. So all their plans had come to nothing!

'Yes,' the man went on, 'four of us at your service – ready to tie you and your little friends up nicely. Well, children, so you thought you'd help our prisoners to escape, did you? I'm afraid we have nasty suspicious natures – and we're a good deal more cunning than you are!'

'Cunning or not,' said George, furiously, 'you're kidnappers and spies, and *that*'s nothing to be proud of!'

'Now, now, my lad, you hold your tongue, or I'm afraid we'll have to gag you. And you won't like that a bit, will you?'

'You leave my cousin Georgina alone or you'll be sorry!' shouted Dick.

'Well, well! Just listen to him!' said the man. 'So your talkative cousin is a girl, is she? Too bad! We'll be treating you all the same, girls or boys, and since you seem so keen to keep our prisoners company, you can join them.'

The men were all armed. Julian realised it would be silly to try resisting them. 'Keep still, George!' he told his cousin softly. 'And you too, Dick. Don't cry, Anne!'

Anne was shedding floods of silent tears. Poor little girl – it wasn't so much that she was frightened on her own account, but she was so sorry the rescue had failed.

'Well, at least *you've* got a bit of sense, my lad!' said the man, laughing. 'We're going to tie you all up, but I trust you'll soon be free again.'

'All depending what sort of reply the Government gives to CHECK's ultimatum,' his accomplice explained.

And as he and the other man talked, he was busy tying the four cousins up one by one.

George wondered where Timmy had got to. She couldn't see him anywhere. She only hoped he wasn't going to try attacking the spies on his own – they all had guns!

Before so very long she knew where he was. The second of the two spies had just finished tying up Julian, Dick and Anne, and he moved on to George herself. The moment he laid a hand on her, a shape shot out of the darkness – and the man howled!

He had just got a nasty bite in a very well-cushioned part of himself!

'Ouch! Ow! Ouch!' he cried, letting go of George.

She thought she might be able to take advantage of this distraction to run for it – but the other man gave her no chance. He grabbed her and held her tight. Furious, George saw the man Timmy had attacked turn on the dog and bring his pistol butt down on Timmy's head. Timmy sank to the ground without so much as a whine, and lay there motionless.

'Oh, you brute!' You've *killed* him!' cried George.

'You be quiet, or *you'll* be for it,' said the man angrily. 'So much for this filthy beast of yours!' And he gave poor Timmy a savage kick, and then picked up his limp body and threw it into a bramble bush.

Poor George! She could hardly see for her tears, let alone put up any sort of fight when she was tied up in her turn. It was too much to bear!

The men left Timmy where he was, and carried the helpless children into the fort. A few minutes later they found themselves being put roughly down beside the Kolkovs, who were tightly tied up too. It was very depressing. The men made sure the bars were still in place, and took away the metal files. They left their prisoners there in the dark. There was only the moon to cast a little light into the gloomy dungeon.

'We're in a nice mess now!' muttered Julian – speaking for everyone.

'Oh dear!' sighed Professor Kolkov. 'To think you four brave children are in such danger just because of us!'

'Don't bother about that, sir!' said Dick

earnestly. 'It's the other way round – *you* might well be cross with *us*! If only we'd gone straight to the police instead of trying to rescue you ourselves, you might be free at this very moment!'

Julian told the Kolkovs the story of what had happened at Kirrin Cottage. He described the arrest of the two imposters, Zekov and Rakin, and the discovery of Alex's message on the handkerchief in the ruins of Corrie Castle. Dick and Anne added a few remarks. As for the Kolkovs, they told the children their own story, and said how happy and hopeful they had been when 'Miss Kirrin' dropped the knife into their prison that afternoon.

Just at the moment 'Miss Kirrin' wasn't saying anything. Dick was the first to notice how quiet his cousin was, and he guessed why.

'Don't worry, old girl!' he told her. 'Timmy's got a good solid skull! I'm sure he isn't dead.'

'Timmy?' said the Professor, in alarm. 'Is there another of you? Is somebody wounded?'

'Timmy's my – my dog,' said George, sniffing. 'And – and those horrible men *hit* him just now! *He* was helping to rescue you, too.'

'Honestly, George, he's got a good thick skull!' Dick repeated, trying to cheer her up. But George sniffed harder than ever.

'If he wasn't dead he'd be back at the window by now, to let us know he was here,' she said sadly.

'He may just be unconscious,' said Julian. 'The

cool night air will soon bring him round again, and then I know he'll try to join us!'

'Yes – and next time they really *will* kill him. Poor old Timmy! He was such a dear, faithful, loving dog!'

There was no comforting George! For once she didn't mind who saw her crying. It was such an unusual sight that her cousins were horrified and couldn't think what to say. They were almost in tears over old Timmy themselves.

'I'm dreadfully sorry,' murmured the Professor.

Alex realised it was no use trying to cheer George up, and they had better change the subject. There wasn't much time, either, if they were to have any hope of escape. He was wriggling frantically in his bonds.

'We don't know your dog is dead,' he told George. 'In fact, we'll have to get out of here before we can find out. We'd better cut ourselves free to start with!'

Everybody looked at him in the moonlight, baffled.

Alex smiled. 'Yes, that is what I said!' he told them. 'In all the excitement, the men from CHECK forgot to pick up George's knife. I managed to push it under my mattress with my foot.'

He wriggled a bit more, and finally managed to get hold of the knife where he had hidden it.

Grasping it in his bound hands, he said, 'I've got it! Now, who's going to try it first?'

Dick had rolled over to Alex's side, and was already rubbing the rope tying his wrists together against the blade of the knife. He worked away so hard that he was soon free. Next moment he had cut the ropes around his feet, and then he moved on to free the others.

As soon as *he* was free, Julian went over to the window. They had cut a little way through the bars, but unfortunately they still held.

'I know what,' said George. 'Let's tie a rope to one of them, and we'll all pull together.'

Dick tied a rope to one of the bars, and the six prisoners all pulled hard. Almost at once they found themselves lying in a heap on the floor! The bar itself hadn't broken – but it had come out of the place where it was set into the wall. Luckily it hadn't made much noise. Very helpfully, it had fallen on Alex's mattress instead of on the floor, where it would have made a loud clang.

This was very encouraging, 'Oh, do let's try one of the other two bars!' said Anne.

'But don't let's pull quite so hard this time,' George advised them. 'We don't want to attract our jailers' attention by making a lot of noise.'

But the second bar was not as ready to come out as the first had been. They couldn't get anywhere with it to begin with, but eventually their united efforts shifted it out of place. That meant that a medium-sized man could get through easily enough – and thus a child could get through without any trouble at all.

George and Dick were the first to clamber out. They were both very supple and athletic. Julian, Anne and Alex followed them. Finally, they managed to haul Professor Kolkov himself out. So there they were, all six of them, out in the open air under the light of the moon.

'We can't stay here!' said the Professor. 'Those men will soon find out we're gone.'

'We've got four bicycles,' said Julian, who had been thinking fast. 'You and your son and my sister and my cousin had better take them, sir. Go and find shelter and alert the police as fast as you can! My brother and I will follow you, cutting across as fast as *we* can!'

'No, all the rest of you go,' said George. 'You can take Anne on your carrier, Julian. I'm staying here! I'm not going to leave without Timmy.'

'Don't be silly, George!' said Julian. 'Every minute counts. Listen, we'll come back and look for Timmy.'

'I'm not leaving without him,' said George obstinately.

'Then I'm staying too,' said Dick. 'Let's try and find him, and if he's still alive we'll take him with us!'

The two Kolkovs exchanged glances. 'You go, Father,' Alex said. 'It's you they really want – we can't risk *your* freedom! I'm going to stay with George and Dick.'

'Julian, you go with the Professor and take Anne with you,' Dick insisted. 'You can come back with help, and meanwhile we'll look for Timmy!'

While they were all talking in whispers, George had plunged into the bramble bush where the spy had left poor Timmy. But search as she might, she couldn't find her dog.

'Oh no!' she muttered to herself. 'Can they have come back for his body and thrown it in the sea? Or did he come round and drag himself off somewhere to die?'

She started searching farther afield. The Kolkovs and her cousins were still arguing about who should go and who should stay. Suddenly, they heard shouts of fury inside the fort. They all froze! The men from CHECK must have discovered that their prisoners had escaped.

'It's too late now!' said Julian in an undertone. 'We ought to have run for it straight away – we're done for!'

All the same, he started making for the place where they had left the bicycles, and everyone except George followed him.

However, they hadn't even got to the camping place before the four spies were after them! And what could they do against four armed men

At this moment George suddenly heard a sound. *She* had stayed behind, hiding in the dark. All of a sudden a smile of delight appeared on her face!

'*Timmy*!' she whispered.

She heard it again – a faint barking. 'Woof! Woof!'

It was coming from the far side of the meadow, where it sloped down to the cliff path. Taking no notice at all of the prickles scratching her, George bravely made her way through the gorse as fast and quietly as she could. Once she got to the path, something soft and warm jumped right into her arms. It was Timmy himself!

He licked her face all over – and suddenly George realised there were shadowy figures standing all around her. She recognised her father and the Police Inspector, with several of his men.

'Father – oh, *Father*! I'm so glad to see you,' she cried, flinging herself into Uncle Quentin's arms.

'Hush, my dear,' said Uncle Quentin. 'We came by car, but we thought we'd better come up to the fort on foot, so we left our vehicles a little way off.'

'But how . . . ?' George began.

'Well, it was Timmy who raised the alarm,' said Uncle Quentin. 'He turned up with blood on his poor nose, a big bump on his head, in fact in such a poor way that your mother and I were really alarmed. But Timmy wouldn't even let us look at his wounds or give him a drink – he led me to the road and kept looking back to make sure I was following him. So I guessed that all you children must be in trouble, and I rang the police at once. Then we came here! Exhausted as he was, Timmy followed us. But what *is* going on, George? You're in quite a state yourself! Your clothes are all torn, and your face and arms are scratched and bleeding. And where are the others?'

'Up there – with the Kolkovs – trying to get away from CHECK!' said George, a little faintly.

'*What?*' cried Uncle Quentin and the policemen all at once.

'I'll explain it all later – and but for Timmy, it might have been too late to explain *anything*! Oh, quick – we must help them!' cried George. 'But do be careful – the spies have guns!'

The Inspector whispered something to his men, and they moved forward in silence. What a wonderful catch this would be for him!

They struck so quickly and unexpectedly – and so efficiently, too – that the four men from CHECK, who were busy overpowering their prisoners again, never even had time to realise what was happening! They were very soon disarmed, and put in handcuffs. The Law had won, all along the line! Such a setback meant that the CHECK spy ring would never survive.

Dawn was rising over the sea when the policemen, Uncle Quentin, the Five, the Kolkovs and the spies left the fort and set off for Kirrin. The spies were put into cells at the police station for the time being. Uncle Quentin, the Five and the Kolkovs went back to Kirrin Cottage, where Aunt Fanny was waiting very anxiously. Professor Kolkov and Alex told her about all that the children had done for them. But Uncle Quentin cut their praises short and said everybody had better go to bed. 'There'll be plenty of time to discuss it all later,' he said.

Before she went upstairs, however, George turned to everyone, beaming, and said, 'Actually if anyone deserves a medal, it's Timmy! As soon as he came round he knew he had to go for help! I tell you what – my dog is cleverer than all the spies from CHECK put together!'

And nobody felt like contradicting her.

If you have enjoyed this book you may like to read some more exciting adventures from Knight Books:

ENID BLYTON

A complete list of the FAMOUS FIVE adventures:

1. Five on a Treasure Island
2. Five go Adventuring Again
3. Five Run Away Together
4. Five go to Smuggler's Top
5. Five go off in a Caravan
6. Five on Kirrin Island Again
7. Five go off to Camp
8. Five get into Trouble
9. Five fall into Adventure
10. Five on a Hike Together
11. Five have a Wonderful Time
12. Five go down to the Sea
13. Five go to Mystery Moor
14. Five have Plenty of Fun
15. Five on a Secret Trail
16. Five go to Billycock Hill
17. Five get into a Fix
18. Five on Finniston Farm
19. Five go to Demon's Rocks
20. Five have a Mystery to Solve
21. Five are Together Again

KNIGHT BOOKS

WILLARD PRICE

A complete list of his thrilling animal adventures:

1. Amazon Adventure
2. South Sea Adventure
3. Underwater Adventure
4. Volcano Adventure
5. Whale Adventure
6. African Adventure
7. Elephant Adventure
8. Safari Adventure
9. Lion Adventure
10. Gorilla Adventure
11. Diving Adventure
12. Cannibal Adventure
13. Tiger Adventure
14. Arctic Adventure

Hal and Roger Hunt are sent all over the world by their father in search of rare animals with which to supply zoos. Their adventures on the way are full of action and suspense and every book is packed with information about the remoter regions of the earth, together with encyclopaedic facts about the world's animal kingdom.

NICHOLAS FISK

THE STARSTORMER SAGA

Starstormers
Sunburst
Catfang
Evil Eye
Volcano

The four Starstormers are Vawn, Ispex, Tsu and Makenzi. They construct a spaceship from pieces of scrap and, together with their robot Shambles, take off into deepest space. *Starstormer* takes them into a thrilling series of space adventures, including strange encounters on alien planets and a continual and dangerous battle against the wicked Octopus Emperor.

KNIGHT BOOKS